THE ORDINARY MONSTER

MARIO KIEFER

mariokiefer.com

Lego ergo sum. Scribo ergo sum.

ISBN 978-0-578-47848-7

For Ric, always.

PROLOGUE

There was no doubt about it; the man was evil — deserving of the death penalty. The man had no compassion for his victim, no kindness for those around him. Had it gone to trial, the jury most assuredly would have returned a guilty verdict. But no such verdict was made. No sentence was ever issued or carried out. The son of the victim had other plans, and, before the man could face the consequences of his actions, took justice into his own hands.

On the day the man was laid to rest, crowds gathered outside the gates of the cemetery in celebration of his death. These crowds were friends and supporters of the victim.

"*Justice!*" they cried.

It seemed very odd, indeed, that those who cried out for justice did not understand the difference between their goal and vengeance. Stranger still was the fact that the man's crime was the result of his own misguided attempt to find that much vaulted justice. He, too, had not understood that his own need for vengeance was not really justice at all. It was ironic that the crowds did not see that parallel as they rejoiced in the man's death.

I stood nearby the man's gravesite as they lowered his body into his final resting place and watched the very small gathering of mourners.

I looked to the man's mother and saw the stony face of anguish. Here was a woman who knew of the evils her son had perpetrated, but still mourned the loss of her child.

I looked to the man's wife and saw the silent tears that rolled down her cheek. Here was a woman who knew that the man had committed a horrendous crime, but who still mourned the loss of a husband.

I looked at the face of his child; a young boy who would never understand what evil his father had wrought; a young boy who did not care. All the child knew was that his father was gone — he had a daddy no more.

And as I listened to the rejoicing outside the cemetery gates; as I stared into the eyes of the men and women demanding justice, I considered what I knew of this man's life.

CHAPTER 1

The old man prayed.

"Oh, most merciful God! Prostrate at your feet, I implore Your forgiveness. I sincerely desire to leave all my evil ways and to confess my sins with all sincerity to You and to Your priest. I am a sinner, have mercy on me, Oh Lord. Give me a lively faith and a firm hope in the Passion of my Redeemer. Give me, for Your mercy's sake a sorrow for having offended so good a God. Mary, my mother, refuge of sinners, pray for me that I may make a good confession. Amen."

He continued as he genuflected inside the confessional. "In the name of the Father, and of the Son and of the Holy Spirit, bless me, Father, for I have sinned. It has been . . . well, so long since my last confession that I cannot remember when I made it."

"Proceed," the priest said from behind the grate.

"Where do I begin?" he asked, more to himself than to the priest and as he did so, he looked down at his hands still folded in prayer. The glint of his wedding band caught his attention and momentarily distracted him from the task before him as his thoughts wandered to his wife, and he wondered, "What am I doing? What chaos will this cause? Will she be able to forgive me?"

"Start from the beginning," the priest prodded.

"The beginning," the old man harrumphed and thought, "what's the beginning? In a life as long as mine and filled with as many sins as there are days, where is there to begin?"

He looked back down at his hands and noticed the small wrinkles on the back and wondered, "When did I get so old? How has so much time passed?"

To the priest, he said, "Tonight, I confronted a monster, but the story of my sins go back so long ago. Back before you were even born, *Padre* — when I was still a young man. My sins have spanned these many decades, but the beginning; well, the beginning, I suppose, was that early morning in 1961 — the morning I first met *La Furia*. To tell you my sins, I have to start way back then."

"*La Furia?*"

Ignoring the priest's question, the old man wondered aloud, "Is there a Commandment that I have not broken?"

Then to the priest, he said, "I guess we can begin with them. On that morning, I placed another above the Lord. I worshipped at the altar of a false god when I turned to *La Furia*. I took His name in vain. Those are the first two."

Although the old man could not see it, the priest furrowed his brow and asked, "And, how did you do that?"

The old man stared down at his wedding band once again. He

began to fiddle with that ring twisting it around his finger as he became lost in the memories of that day — the day that had started it all.

Hector had been watching Jesús all morning. The older man was working hard, harvesting. He continued the back-breaking work, up and down row after row of cotton plants. Down those rows, Hector clearly saw Jesús's family as well — at least the ones that were old enough to work in the fields. Like their father, these *niños* toiled just as hard.

At this time, the heat of the day had risen as quickly as the sun that now stood almost directly overhead. Soon, it would be time to break. Hector looked forward to the respite from his work, not because he did not enjoy the work, but because he knew that break meant that he would be able to investigate his suspicions; the suspicions that had been invading his mind these past few weeks without relent. It did not matter how often or how hard he tried to push them away, they came to him insisting upon his attention in much the same way that a germaphobe with obsessive compulsive disorder might constantly wash his hands.

Hector could not get the thoughts out of his mind. These thoughts drove him to such distraction that he found it more than a little difficult to continue with the harvest. As the morning wore on, he found himself looking from his satchel of cotton to Jesús, and then to the rows ahead, and back to Jesús again.

When finally, the field boss called for a halt so that the men may take their lunch, Hector dropped his satchel and hoe to the ground, and watched Junior, Jesús's eldest boy, scurry off to sit under a tree and eat — no doubt Fabia had packed him a lunch of *frijoles taquitos* again. Junior would, of course, complain that he was still hungry after he finished that meal. Hector's own lunch would go untouched by him, because today, he had other plans.

As the *braceros* began their meal, he spied Jesús walk down the little trail toward the shacks. He lingered behind to give the other man time to get well ahead of him, before he sauntered off in the same direction. But before he did, he paused to give to Junior the wrapped *torta* that was his own lunch. Hector was not hungry, after all, and Junior was more than ecstatic by the gift.

As he came to the clearing where his own home stood, Hector paused and watched Jesús enter the door; the door that was answered by Hector's very own wife, Mariana. He moved away from the clearing, just to the edge, but well out of sight, and stood behind a large oak tree that grew some forty yards away from the door to his home.

Reaching into his pack of tobacco, he rolled a cigarette and stood, watching that door. There was no breeze to speak of since the air was very still, and, although the canopy of the tree provided some protection from the sun, sweat poured from Hector's brow. Still, he knew that sweat was not from the heat of the day, rather its source was the heat that rose in his belly; a fire that he was not certain he could douse.

He reached up and wiped his forehead with the little cotton handkerchief that had been a gift from his wife — the very same wife that now was behind the closed door of his home with another man — before he rolled a new cigarette from his tobacco and continued chain-smoking as he watched the door to his little shack.

More than once, Hector started toward the door of his home, but each time he did so, he only found himself returning to his spot under the tree. If one watched from a distance, one might conclude that he was simply pacing back and forth as he continued to smoke, cigarette after cigarette, looking much like an expectant father in the waiting room of a hospital for news of the birth of his heir. But this was no hospital maternity ward. This was no place of joy. This was the clearing around which stood the bunkhouse for the *braceros* as well as the few little shacks that were provided for the men who brought their families with them to work these fields.

The clearing formed a circle around a campfire at its center. In the evening hours, the men who toiled in these fields gathered to sing, talk, and drink the day's labors away. Hector's mind flashed to the many nights he sat in that clearing with the *braceros* and his friend, Jesús, recalling the hours deep in conversation; conversations that ranged from philosophical questions to absurd and bawdy jokes. How he always laughed at Jesús's many jokes — especially the double-entendres. Jesús was a master story-teller and each and every one of the men loved to hear him spin a yarn. After all of these years, how was Hector to have known that he was one of the characters in so many of Jesús's tales? How was he to know that he had been the butt of the jokes?

He knew that Jesús had a roving eye, everyone knew, but could not really understand the reason. Jesús's wife, Fabia, was a beautiful woman and (at least according to Jesús) always willing to give in to her husband's desires. Why then did the older man seek pleasure in the arms of other women? Was Hector's friend so driven by fleshly pursuits that he did not understand the difference between making sex and making love? Was he even capable of such an understanding?

Even knowing this about his friend, Hector never thought that Jesús would pursue his own wife. There were some lines that no man was meant to cross. What kind of man would so dishonor his very close *amigo* after or during so many years of such a friendship?

In time, Hector saw Jesús exit the house and witnessed the quick little brush of the lips that his own wife planted onto those of his erstwhile friend. He watched as Jesús looked around while placing his straw cowboy hat atop his head before turning toward the trail that led back to the fields.

Deep within, he felt the fire burn, and, in that moment, he wanted nothing more than to chase after Jesús and immediately confront him. But despite the conflagration that threatened to engulf his very being, he steeled himself.

He stubbed out his cigarette on the heel of his boot and walked down the little trail that led back to the fields, being careful to remain far enough behind that Jesús would never know that he had seen.

In those fields, the lunch hour was over and the *braceros* were returning to the harvest. Hector watched as Jesús spoke with another man. That man clapped Jesús on the back and then howled in laughter. Jesús, the master storyteller, must have told the man a very good tale, indeed, and in that moment, Hector knew. He knew the plot of this particular story and who its main characters must be.

Hector's face flushed red with shame; the shame that a man feels when he knows that he has been cuckolded by his wife; the shame a man feels when he is aware that everyone around him also knows; the shame a man feels when he realizes that he had been blind to the true intentions of his *friend.*

A burning anger accompanied that flush of shame on its march from his belly to his face and, without even knowing what he was doing, Hector reached out and picked up the hoe that he had previously discarded on the ground. He did not think about why he had picked up that instrument. His mind was empty of thought and his heart devoid of feeling. He did not see the rays of sun that streaked down from the sky and alit upon his shoulders. Although, he did not see that light, he felt the heat; but the heat he felt did not emanate from those rays, rather they came from deep within him. Nor did he consider what he was doing as he quickened his pace toward Jesús and the other man. His body moved forward of its own volition and without his command. In his mind's eye, Hector sat far away watching the events unfold and wondered what he was doing.

When Hector was but yards away from the two men, Junior ran across his path and blocked his passage.

"*Padrino,*" Junior said, "*gracias por la comida*. I was so hungry and that filled me up. I don't know how to thank you. I am always so hungry!"

Hector stopped short and looked down at the newly minted teenager in front of him not recognizing the boy. He had no idea who this child was and did not understand what he was saying, but then the heat that had overtaken him dissipated almost as quickly as it had risen. He looked down at his hand to the hoe that he held and dropped it to the ground before looking back to the boy. Junior's face returned into focus and his words once again became intelligible.

With a nervous smile, he tousled the boy's hair. "*De nada,*" he said. "I was not hungry. Besides, a growing boy needs to eat far more than I do."

Junior smiled up at his godfather then scampered away back to the field and to the harvest; back to where the boy's father now stooped pulling the bolls of cotton from their bracts. Hector watched the boy as he did so until he caught sight of his "friend," then his eyes narrowed, and he reached down, picked up the hoe and his own bag. He moved to a different row of cotton to continue his work.

CHAPTER 2

In the confessional, the old man said, "Thirty-years ago, I caught my wife, Mariana, with another man. That man was my best friend, *mi hermano*, my brother, or so I thought. That was the day that *La Furia* was conceived. That was the day that I broke the First and Second Commandments.

"Before then, I had always been a happy man, you see. Naturally, there were the small irritations that each and every man must face, and God, Himself, knows that I had my share, but I had never been truly angry before — not like that. On that day, I was consumed by hate and rage; so much hate and so much anger; at my wife and also at *mi amigo*." He said these last two words with an ironic lilt and a little sneer.

He continued, "In truth, at that point, I was angry at everything and everyone. I was lost, you see. And, I have been lost since that day. I may have learned to control the anger, but it has never really gone away. *La Furia* was conceived on that day and she has followed me ever since, but she wasn't fully born until the next morning."

"What happened then?" the priest asked.

The old man looked down at his hands again and silently considered.

Throughout the remainder of that afternoon, Hector worked the field trying his best to keep his distance from Jesús, but the other man often managed to find his way back to Hector's side. While they continued the arduous work at hand, they made small talk and told jokes. For his part, Hector smiled and tried to laugh at Jesús's little jokes, but deep inside he felt no mirth. His laughter was no more than his attempt to hide the teeming anger that threatened to engulf him from within.

As Jesús continued his inane chatter, Hector's mind continually returned to the image of Jesús at the front door of his home. In these visions, the other man wore a self-satisfied grin; the type of smile that evil men wore when they had completed an evil deed.

He imagined himself taking the hoe that he held in his hands and smashing it into the smile that his "friend" now wore. He managed to maintain control of his ever-growing anger. But as the sun was dragged further to the West, Hector felt that if Jesús did not cease his constant chatter, he just might lose that discipline.

Finally, the field boss called for a halt to the work for the day and released the *braceros* to return to their homes. Hector took his bag of cotton to the scales to be weighed and measured.

"I don't think that I have done too well today, my friend," Jesús said as the pair walked to the scales. "I may need another loan this week to get some food for the children."

Hector looked over to Jesús and grunted in a non-committal

manner. For his part, Jesús took this to be assent for Hector had never before denied him.

"*Gracias*," Jesús said. "Are you coming to the campfire? I have some good stories for tonight."

"No," Hector replied curtly, "Mariana is ill again, and I need to go back to see her." As he said this, Hector carefully watched Jesús to gauge the level of his guilt or shame, but in Jesús's eyes, he saw none.

"Ah," Jesús responded. "I understand. She is ill often and I know that you want to take care of her in the way that a husband should."

Hector was amazed that he was able to stay his hand under the provocation of that comment. Every fiber of his being called out for him to punch his friend in the face. Whether Jesús meant it or not, Hector took the comment as an affront against his manhood. In Hector's mind, Jesús was saying that since he, Hector, was not 'taking care of' his woman, Jesús had taken it upon himself to do so.

Rather than reply, Hector gave his friend a tight smile, took the little sheet of paper that the field boss handed him indicating his daily take, then turned and walked back toward his home.

Jesús looked after his friend as the boss weighed his sack wondering why Hector was acting so strangely. For the next several minutes he watched until Hector turned the corner of the trail and he could see him no more.

It was not long before Hector arrived at his home. He stopped at its threshold where the ghost of his "friend" stood wearing that terrible grin. When he entered, he woke Mariana from her nap.

"*Lo siento, Hector*," his wife apologized. "*Tengo la migraña, otro vez*," she said to her husband.

"*Pobrecita*," Hector responded. "your migraines seem to come frequently these days. What do you do to reduce the stress?"

"Yes," she replied. "They come all of the time, now. The only thing to be done is to rest."

"It's ok. I am not hungry. Rest, I can fend for myself."

Hector grabbed a *tortilla* from the counter next to the stove, spread some butter on it then went outside. He sat on the front porch of his home and, after eating his dinner, rolled a cigarette from his pack of tobacco.

To the priest, the old man replied, "I said nothing to Jesús that afternoon. Instead, I tried to avoid him, but despite my efforts to work in another part of the field, he always managed to be near me. Whether he realized that I was trying to avoid him, I can't really say.

"Throughout the rest of that afternoon, I continued to work, but the anger inside me grew with each passing hour. It grew with each plant that I harvested. By the end of the day, I was tired and angrier than ever. When Jesús asked me to come out for a drink, I told him that I could not. Mariana had been ill, I said, and I needed to go home.

"And, when I got home, I said nothing to Mariana that evening. She knew that something was wrong, but I did not tell her what I had seen. Instead, as I had done all day in the fields, I pretended only to have the harvest on my mind.

"I told my wife to go to bed without me, and, so, she did. There was no way that I was going to slip into that bed next to her. How could I lie down in that bed? How could I place the blanket of her betrayal on top of me? How could I lay next to a lie? No, there was no way that I was going to bed with her. The mattress had the stench of her betrayal.

"So, I sat on the front step, smoking my cigarettes and thinking. I thought about my life with Mariana. I thought about my friendship with that *cabrón*, Jesús."

Quickly, he apologized, "Sorry, Padre, I did not mean to use profanity. I guess that we should add that to my list of sins."

Once again, he became lost in thought.

Hector sat on his front steps smoking. He thought about what Jesús and Mariana had done; how they had betrayed him. As he thought, the anger and hatred simmered within. Ever so slowly, it simmered, until it began to boil.

He had no idea how long he sat there, but it was very early in the morning before he moved from that spot. His tobacco was gone and although he had not eaten anything except for a single *tortilla* since breakfast the morning before, he was not hungry. Instead, he was nauseated. The thought of eating anything that may have been prepared by his wife's cheating hands only made him feel more so. But morning crept upon him and there was the new day's harvest to consider.

When he rose and went inside, he did so with the full intention of cleaning himself and returning to work; that is, until he stole into the bedroom and saw her.

His wife was sleeping like a baby; as if she had no care in the world. She just slept in peace until she opened her eyes, looked at him, and smiled — that same beautiful smile that he had fallen in love with years ago; that same beautiful smile that once had stolen his heart; that same beautiful smile that now had stolen the truth; the very same smile that hid her lies.

CHAPTER 3

"That's when it happened."

"What happened?" the priest asked.

"I felt it inside. Something . . . broke, *Padre*; like a stick that has been pushed and pulled this way and that way until finally it cracks then snaps in two. And, when it does, it does it suddenly and without warning. One moment, you have that whole stick in your hands and the next moment you are holding two broken pieces.

"It felt as if I were thrown from my body and my spirit stood there next to the now empty shell watching the two pieces of that stick, one flesh and one not.

"I lost sight of God at that moment and through the gash that had been made when the parts were rent, *La Furia* entered and took control. I couldn't stop her. I couldn't do anything, I was just . . . air.

"If the truth is told, though, I didn't even try to stop her. I let her in. I allowed that false god to turn me away from the real one. And, I watched as she drove my body to the other room and retrieved my gun."

"*Dios mio*," the priest whispered.

"Oh, *Padre*," Hector continued. "God was not there that morning; only Mariana, *La Furia*, and me. That is when I broke the Fifth Commandment."

Hector heard Mariana rise and don her housecoat. He knew that she was coming to make *desayuno,* but he was in no mood to breakfast. He wanted to call to her; to tell her not to come. He wanted her to stay far away. But *La Furia* had full control of his body and he could not cry out. All that he could do was watch as his wife entered the kitchen.

Mariana smiled at him. "My migraine is gone and I am feeling much better," she said. "I will make you some *huevos con frijoles*."

Hector, or rather the thing that now controlled him, silently sat at the table and watched — holding his gun in his lap hidden beneath the table and well out of sight of the woman standing in front of the stovetop. He tried to wrench his hand free. He wanted to throw the gun away from him, but no matter how ardently his mind commanded, his hand would not obey.

"Poor thing," Mariana said. "You look as if you have had no sleep. Did you come to bed at all? I must have been dead to the world, I never heard you come in."

Hector wanted to scream to her, "Get out! Run!" but his voice betrayed him and when he opened his mouth he did not speak the words that he intended. Instead, he heard his voice ask, "Did you see Jesús yesterday?"

Mariana turned toward him furrowing her brow, "What makes you ask that? Of course, I didn't see him. He was out in the fields with you all day, and I was here nursing my headache."

She looked at him quizzically for a moment, then turned her back to him as she pulled the frying pan from the hook where it hung above the stove.

With her back to him she continued, "Fabia didn't even stop by after I told her that I was ill. I spent the day alone."

"Liar!" he wanted to scream, but held his tongue. Hector's fingers twitched and his hand began to shake as he tried desperately to wrest control from the demon that had possessed him. In a blink of an eye, he spent hours struggling for control, and then, from far away, he listened as he heard himself say, "Strange; I thought that I saw him come this way around lunchtime."

"He must have gone to see Fabia," Mariana replied keeping her back to him as she cracked open two eggs and watched them hit the pan. They sizzled as the heat from the pan turned their edges white.

By no command of his own, but at the insistence of *La Furia*, Hector stood toppling the chair to the floor behind him. Then *La Furia* used his very own hand to point the gun at his wife.

Surprised by the noise of the falling chair, Mariana turned to Hector. When she saw the barrel of that gun pointed at her, her eyes widened.

Again, Hector tried to wrench that hand free from the control of *La Furia*, but he could not. The demon's control was complete. He could do nothing as he watched his own hand, the hand that he no longer controlled, the one that was now controlled by, perhaps, Satan himself, pull the trigger.

Three times, that trigger was pulled and Hector watched as his wife's smile finally disappeared.

"*Dios mio*," the priest proclaimed again.

"The monster wasn't done yet, *Padre*. Not by a long shot. Mariana was gone, but Jesús was still out there. So, I watched from far away as *La Furia* reloaded the gun and stole into the morning to find him."

The monster drove Hector's body down the path that led to Jesús's house, while Hector's spirit could only follow bound by some unseen tether and unable to wrench control away from the demon that possessed it. When he approached the door of the two-room shack, he halted and listened to the stirrings of the family within and the sounds they made as they rose and prepared for the day.

Hector heard the children move about while dressing. He heard Fabia bark orders to Luciana as the girl prepared the breakfast; and he heard Luciana's complaints to her younger brother to get out of her way. From within the house, he heard the sound of the baby cry followed by the cooing sounds that Luciana made to calm the child.

Soon, Jesús would sit to breakfast; a breakfast prepared by his daughter, but served by his wife, Fabia, as she had done each and every morning since their first day together as husband and wife.

He wondered whether Fabia had any inkling about their respective spouses' dirty secret. Jesús's wife was no fool. There was no doubt that she knew of her husband's other indiscretions. How could she not have known about Mariana? Then again, had she known, would she and Mariana have remained so close?

Luciana gathered the baby, little Gus, into her arms, and handed to him the ordinary doll that Mariana had given to the children for Christmas just last year; the doll with the red and white striped legs. He remembered the excitement of the children at this gift; as small as it was.

As he watched the family through the window, he felt the rage within begin to ebb. As it did, he thought that he might yet wrench control of his body from *La Furia* and turn away. He considered that he might run from this place before the demon could do more damage. But, before he could make the move to retake his body, Jesús entered the room and sat at the table. Through Hector's eyes, the demon watched Fabia serve her husband and the rage consumed him. *La Furia* assumed complete control and any hope he had of evicting the demon from its chosen vessel faded away.

Helpless, Hector watched from within himself, unable to stop the monster as it drove his body. The physical shell that was Hector crashed through the door, and the man that was imprisoned within could do nothing to stop the monster. It raised the gun and fired, reaping vengeance on his behalf.

Jesús (the coward!) dove under the table before that first bullet had left its chamber enraging the demon further who then blindly shot into the room.

Hector watched as Jesús's daughter, Luciana, fell to the floor, and from the corner of his eye, he saw the ordinary doll that the baby held tumble into a pool of the girl's blood.

He heard the cries of the other children as they hid under their blankets.

He heard Jesús's son, Junior, scream in pain, when in slow motion the cast iron pot of beans trapped the boy's hand between it and the flames of the stove's burners. Unable to do anything else, he watched as Fabia wrenched the boy's hand from under that cast iron pot.

The boy howled again, and, at that moment, Hector felt *La Furia* leave his body while his own spirit returned. He looked down the length of his arm to his hand — the very hand that just now had hurt these *niños* — and was surprised to find that it still held the gun. He looked up from that hand and saw the family crouched in terror.

Even as he heard their cries, he still could not believe what he had done.

Hector wanted to shout, "It's not my fault! It wasn't me! I swear that I did not do this! It was the monster; the demon that had taken control; the one that had driven my body!"

But no words passed his lips.

As Hector looked on, he saw the shadow that was *La Furia*; the evil that had left his body. He watched in horror as it crossed the room then entered into Junior's through the bloody nubs that had once been fingers.

For only the briefest of moments, Junior stopped screaming. The boy looked toward his *padrino* and in his eyes, Hector clearly saw that Junior was no longer there. From the eyes of the child, *La Furia* stared back at him, and despite the immense pain that the boy's body must have been in, the demon inside the boy drove Junior's lips to smile at the vessel it had just departed.

"So, there you have it, *Padre*. Commandments 1, 2, and 5 broken in one fell swoop.

"I broke those Commandments. I turned to a false god and let her lead me astray and away from our Lord. At her urging, I murdered my wife and attacked my friend. At her urging, I wounded his children.

"For so many years, I have proclaimed my innocence and blamed *La Furia* for those events. But if I am to be honest, *Padre*, she did not come from nowhere.

"It was in my anger that she was conceived. And it was in my rage that she was born.

"Through that anger; through that rage, I invited her."

CHAPTER 4

"What happened to your hand?" the new guy, asked.

"Oh, here we go," Johnny said as the new guy, Tommy, looked at him quizzically.

It was early 1991, and the four workers sat around a small table in the middle of an old honky-tonk that was situated no more than two or three miles from their work. The table was unbalanced since one of its four legs was shorter than the others and whenever one of the men leaned on the table its wobbling threatened to overturn the pyramid of beer bottles that the men had been slowly building since they first entered this watering hole earlier in the evening. From the look of that pyramid, it was obvious to anyone nearby that these men had already had more than their fair share of the establishment's offerings. It was equally as obvious that these were rough men who used rough hands to work rough jobs in their rough lives. A wayward tourist might do well to stay away from such a lot.

There was nothing special about this particular bar and it was one that had been oft-frequented by the men from the rigs and nearby businesses, that is when those businesses still thrived and had not been hit by the cycle of boom and bust that so epitomized the Texas oil industry in the 1970s, 1980s and even today. The building was small with a maximum occupancy sign that read no more than seventy people were allowed — not that anyone paid attention to that occupancy sign on a Friday or Saturday night when one or more of the local bands came to play. But because this was mid-week, no band was playing and any music that emanated from the establishment came from the tinny speakers of the old jukebox that stood in the far back of the bar next to the cigarette machine that sold those coffin nails for two dollars per pack.

"I am not sure that you want to hear the story. It's very sad" Junior said with a rueful grimace then a glance down at the tabletop.

"Come on," Johnny, the one with the droopy mustache and the piercing green eyes, said, "you might as well tell him. He will only keep asking until you do."

Junior did not know this man, Tommy, the new guy, even so, he was not taken aback by the boldness of the question. These oil workers were generally a blunt lot and if they had a question, they asked. Besides, he had told the story so many times to so many people, he wondered what difference one more time would make. Each of the men with whom he worked had heard the story in one form or another on more than one occasion.

"I guess," Junior thought, "it's time to let the new guy in."

He glanced at the men around him then began his story looking directly at Tommy.

"I lost them when I was very young," he said in almost a whisper.

From the corner of his eye he saw the smirk begin to cross Johnny's face and noted that Daniel kicked him under the table to make sure that he did not interrupt.

"We grew up very poor, you see. My family worked the fields. We went around from place to place picking whatever needed picking. Sometimes, it was oranges and, sometimes, it was corn. Sometimes, it wasn't food at all but other stuff like cotton. None of it was good, but cotton was the worst.

"I was the oldest boy out of twelve children, the third child in the bunch, but the older ones were girls, my sisters, Lucia and Luciana. Lucia wasn't living at home anymore when it happened, though. She had already gone to work in the Big House for the *gringo* who owned the ranch. Sometimes, she would sneak us food from that white man's kitchen, but that didn't happen too often. She had to be very careful when she did that. It wasn't so easy for her to sneak it away. If the *gringo* caught her, well, we would have been fired and forced to leave the ranch."

The new guy sat stonily, engrossed in Junior's story. Maybe not so much by the words that Junior spoke as by the tone that he used when speaking them. His voice was so quiet that Tommy felt as if Junior might actually be reliving the event in the telling and wondered if, perhaps, he should not have asked the question.

"We were poor; so, very poor. We hardly ever had anything to eat except beans, rice, and *tortillas*. That's all we ever had when we had anything at all. I remember a lot of nights we went to bed hungry having had nothing to eat. On those nights, Mama always promised that things would get better and that we would have something to eat in the morning. But, just as often as not, we woke and our breakfast plates were empty just like the ones from dinner the night before; as empty as the promise that she made.

"We worked in the fields and, if we were lucky to be picking something that we could eat, we might sneak some of it away to bring back to the house for dinner. Or, if the stuff from the harvest was not good, the boss didn't care because, as he said, even the dogs would not eat it. There were even times that we were so hungry that Mama made soup out of grass. It wasn't much but it was something."

Tommy listened intently wearing a look of pity that any child might be that hungry.

"I remember that morning on the day that it happened. My sister, Luciana, stood at the stove stirring the grass soup. She was *muy flaca*, you know, very skinny. Her legs were so small that they looked like she was standing on broomsticks — they were that little, I mean. We all were pretty skinny, though. I guess that's what hunger does to you."

At this point, Junior held a far-away look in his eyes and Tommy continued to listen still wearing his look of pity.

"Even the little ones were skinny. Sometimes, when I am watching television late at night and that commercial comes on . . . you know the one, the one with that *pendeja* actress from that show."

"Sally Something-or-Other," Johnny interrupted as if on cue.

"Yeah, that's the one. She is always on TV begging the *güeros* to send money to feed those children in Africa or India or wherever.

"I have to ask, though, what do those white boys care about the kids over there? And, what about the children here? I say. There are plenty of hungry children right here, right now. I know about them. I was one of them. Doesn't that actress care about them? Doesn't she care about us?" Junior's voice had risen in decibel as he railed against that actress — Sally Something-or-Other. But when he returned to his story, his voice softened to not-quite a whisper this time.

"We were like them; my family, I mean. My younger brothers and sisters all had that big *panza*, you know what I mean?" Junior moved his hands around his belly to indicate an enlarged abdomen. "That *panza* that all those starving children seem to have. Why do they have such big bellies if they have no food? It doesn't make any sense to me, but they all do."

"It's *because* of no food, — not even beans and rice," as if on cue, Johnny teasingly interrupted.

"*Cállate*," Daniel tried to silence Johnny. "Let Junior finish the story."

"I don't know," Junior continued, shaking his head. "I only know that my younger sisters all had that. Even so, you could still count their ribs above the belly . . ." waving his left hand, the one with only the thumb and pinky finger, he continued, ". . . one, two, three, four." Junior paused and placed his hands below the table.

"That night, after we had finished the harvest and eaten more grass soup and the baby had finally cried hisself to sleep, Papa pulled me aside. 'The baby has to eat,' he said. 'We all do or we are going to starve to death.' I saw him reach into his front pocket and pull out his pocket-knife. It was the same knife that he used when we were out in the fields and his fingers were too raw and bloody from the poke of the cotton bracts to continue with only his hands."

"What's that?" Tommy asked.

"Cotton bracts? It's the part of the plant that covers the cotton boll."

Junior wrapped his right hand around his balled up left indicating for Tommy to look at them.

"But it's really like the leaves that cover the cotton before it dries. After that it pops open," and he turned his right hand upwards, palm up with fingers splayed out. "It becomes sharp and pricks your hands if you are not wearing gloves — which we couldn't afford and the *gringos* wouldn't give us."

The new guy looked at Junior's good hand, the one with all of its fingers still splayed out in the air, and noticed the little scars that covered them between the tip and the second knuckle.

"Anyway, Papa pulled out his knife and just kept talking about how we were all starving and saying that someone was going to have to make a sacrifice if we were going to survive. I wasn't sure what he meant. What kind of sacrifice? We couldn't put in any more hours in the fields. We were already working from morning to night every day. What more could we do?" Junior looked at his companions pointedly, as if daring them to come up with another idea.

"I was the strongest, he said, so it had to be me to sacrifice. He handed me a bottle of tequila and told me to drink, and to drink a lot. So, I did; and all the while he kept talking about how we were starving and somebody needed to make a sacrifice."

Johnny interrupted, "You couldn't afford food, but you could afford tequila?" he remarked.

"Shhh!" Daniel said, "Let him finish."

Junior reached up with his left hand and began scratching the top of his head with the remaining thumb, then, "He reminded me that it was always the old Aztec way to make a sacrifice when the crops didn't come in, and that we were from strong Aztec blood —

the blood of warriors, he said. Our people, the Aztec, he said, understood about sacrifice. They did what needed doing and these were our people. Like the ones that had come before us, we, too, would do what we needed to do."

When Junior paused for a moment, Tommy watched his face intently. The far-off look in the other man's eyes sent a slight chill down his spine, and he felt the rising goosebumps along his arm.

"As he kept talking about our people and sacrifice, he kept motioning for me to drink more tequila. 'Just keep drinking,' he said. I was only thirteen or fourteen and didn't like the taste. It made me want to throw-up.

"Being so young, it didn't take much to get me good and drunk and when I was, he told me to put my left hand down on the table with all of the fingers out, like this." Junior placed his left hand on the table and spread his thumb and pinky finger wide. From his angle, Tommy could not help but see the wide space between those two fingers where the middle three should have been. His eyes widened as he stared at Junior's hand unable to accept what he was hearing.

"He handed me the bottle of tequila and told me to drink some more, then he put that blade down at the knuckles, right here," and Junior pointed to his hand where the fingers, if he had them, would have extended.

Junior paused for dramatic effect. He took a large swig from his beer, then said, "The next morning, we finally had some meat."

The new guy looked at him in horror until the others at the table roared raucously in laughter.

"You asshole," Tommy said.

Junior grinned and saluted with the beer at his forehead before he pulled that bottle toward his lips to take another swig.

Around the table, the other men continued to talk, but Junior was not really listening as he became lost in thought recalling the real events of that tragic day; the day that had marked him forever.

Thinking on his hunger, thirteen-year old Junior watched as his sister, Luciana, stood at the stove stirring the pot of beans and warming the *tortillas*. He felt, then heard, the rumblings in his belly.

"How much longer?" He asked.

"*¡Ya, basta!*" She replied. "It will be ready when it's ready."

"But, I am hungry now," he insisted. "I can't wait anymore!"

"If you want it so badly, then maybe you should make it yourself," she replied in an irritated voice.

Junior harrumphed at this; as if he, a man, should cook for himself — everyone knew that was woman's work!

"A man needs a full belly to work the fields," he responded.

Luciana looked down at his paunch and nodded, "*Gordito,*" she called him.

Junior laughed and said, "Yeah, I'm fat. I like my *tortillas*! Now hurry up woman and get me my food."

"*Siéntate,*" she replied ordering him to sit down while kicking him in the shin. I will get you some as soon as Papa has his.

And, there it was again. He had to wait for his father, Papa Jesús, to eat. Why did Papa always eat first? What made him so special? The old man always took, took, took, but never gave.

Junior had been very angry with his father ever since that day he found out that Papa Jesús was having an affair with his *madrina,* Mariana. If his mother, Mama Fabia, or Mariana's husband, Hector, knew what was going on, Junior was certain that there would be hell to pay. He did not want to cause any trouble between his parents and his *padrinos.* Nor did he want to cause any trouble within the confines of his own family.

Papa Jesús often said, "*En boca cerrada no entran moscas,*" so, he obeyed. He kept his mouth shut not wanting to let those flies in; not wanting to stir the pot. His family was not just a bunch of beans, after all.

It was just before six a.m. and still dark outside. Soon, the sun would rise and, when it did, he would head to the fields with Papa to bring in the harvest. For now, he watched as his sisters milled around the two-room shack playing with that stupid doll that they had gotten this last Christmas; the little doll with the red-striped legs. He would never understand why the little ones were so entranced with that dumb, little doll.

The baby, Gus, began to cry and Junior watched his sister, Luciana, put him to her shoulder. Even holding the baby, she was able to stir the beans and continue flipping the *tortillas.* Junior marveled that she was able to do all three at the same time knowing, in the stillness of his own heart, that if the roles were reversed, he would be unable to do so.

When he thought about his sister, Junior knew that he loved her more than anything in the world. Naturally, they argued and fought — don't all siblings? Still, he knew in his heart of hearts that there was absolutely nothing he would not do for her; no mountain that he would not climb; and no ocean that he would not cross to protect her from harm. He would even take Papa Jesús's beatings to keep her safe. And he knew that she would do the same for him.

After all, wasn't it Luciana who, when Mama Fabia was angry (and Mama Fabia was always angry) with him over one thing or another, stood up for him and argued with his mother. She did this without care for the consequences that certainly would come.

When he was hungry, it was Luciana who gave him just a little bit more on his plate than was, probably, his fair share. It was Luciana who hid extra food and gave it to him when nobody was looking.

When the other boys in the fields teased him for whatever reason, she was quick to come to his defense and, even if that embarrassed his budding manhood, he was happy to know that she always had his back.

And, when Papa Jesús beat him (as he so often did), it was Luciana that held him and comforted him at night as he stifled his tears.

The brother and sister duo might tease and cajole one another, but it was always from a place of love; a love that came from the bonds of two siblings who endured shared hardship.

Luciana again shooed Junior away, as Papa Jesús entered the room and sat at the head of the table while Mama Fabia placed his breakfast before him; *frijoles*, *huevos* and two *tortillas*. When he was finished eating these beans and eggs, Junior and his siblings would have their turn.

Glancing up at his father, Junior noted the bloodshot eyes and the hoarse hacking in his throat. He knew what this meant . . . Papa Jesús had been drinking with the *braceros* again last night. Not that this was any surprise. Papa Jesús spent most of his nights drinking with the other *borachos* and usually did not return to their home until well after the children had fallen asleep. More often than not, however, Junior remained awake and heard his father stumble into the house. It was not as if the old man tried to sneak in — he was as loud as a dog after a squirrel.

On those nights, Junior kept still and quiet under his blankets at the other side of the dirt-floor room and waited until Papa Jesús finally closed the door to the only other room in their home; the bedroom that his parents shared. Sometimes, after Papa Jesús entered that room, Junior heard the quiet protests of his mother, Mama Fabia, as his father took from his wife what was, after all, a husband's due. On those nights, Junior felt a bitter anger toward his father, but he knew that there was nothing that he could say or do. So, he covered his ears not to hear his mother's complaints or his father's grunts until finally the only sounds emanating from that other room were the quiet tears of his mother and the angry snores of his father.

On this morning, while he waited impatiently to be fed, from outside, he heard two loud bangs and turned his attention to the little window wondering what on earth had made that noise. He paid no attention to the conversation around him as he watched silently from his spot near the old stove. He moved to the window and looked out into the early morning sky, but saw nothing emanating from its darkness. He continued to peer out while giving only half an ear to the conversation going on within the confines of their little shack.

Although he was not paying attention, he heard his father demand the meat this evening and, again, Junior knew what that meant — there would be no meat for him or anyone else. Once again, he would be relegated to eating just the beans and rice that Mama Fabia was sure to make; the beans and rice that they ate on a daily basis after their father had consumed the last of whatever meat there might be. It was a rare occasion, indeed, when the entire family got to partake in that particular fare.

Junior felt a rising anger toward his father; the anger that came whenever Papa Jesús took (at least in Junior's estimation) more than what was his fair share and left the children hungry. But as he so often did, Junior pushed that anger down; way down; as far down as he could. If he let that anger escape and direct itself toward his father, Papa Jesús would be certain to beat him within an inch of his life.

Junior felt the grumbling in his belly again as he thought of the food, and he walked back to the stove and peered into the pot of beans. He whispered to Luciana, "Come on, just give me one *tortilla* now."

"Go away," Luciana whispered. "You're not getting anything until Papa eats."

"Ugh," Junior grunted in response.

Luciana looked over her shoulder at the table where Papa sat, then bent down and whispered into his ear, "I will pack up a little something extra for you for lunch."

Junior smiled at his big sister, then from the corner of his eye, he saw a shadow flit across the window pane. Quickly, he looked up.

"What was that?" he wondered, and squinted toward the darkened window.

He heard Luciana's continued whispers in his ear, but paid them no heed. His entire being concentrated on the window as he saw the shadows outside move again.

". . . candy bar," he heard Luciana say. This caught Junior's attention and he cocked his head to hear her more clearly, momentarily forgetting the shadows outside.

"What?" he asked.

"I have half of a candy bar hidden in my bedding." Luciana repeated *sotto voce*. "When you take me to the outhouse tonight, I will give it to you." Junior's lips widened into a large grin at the prospect of the rich chocolate melting in his mouth.

From outside the front door, he heard a creak. He turned back toward the sound, but heard nothing new. Junior pivoted his head and looked around at his family. Whatever the noise was outside, it had not seemed to register with any of them.

Luciana continued to whisper to him, but he no longer heard anything that she said. A noise that sounded as if someone had dropped something heavy onto the floor came from outside the door.

"*¿Quien es?*" he heard Mama Fabia ask who was there.

Without warning, the door burst in. For a moment, everything was still as the family looked up as one at the entryway where their *padrino,* Hector, stood, arm raised in front of him.

Junior saw the flash of the muzzle before he heard the retort of the bullet leave its chamber. Thereafter, everything moved in slow motion.

He turned toward Luciana who dropped Gus to the floor, then fell back into him. As she did so, she knocked him into the stove. With his right hand, Junior reached out to steady his sister, while with his left hand, he grasped the edge of the stove for purchase. The pot of beans on the stove turned over and spilled its contents onto the floor below. Luciana's foot slipped in the dark brown liquid and she went down.

Junior felt a searing pain in his left hand, then the pressure, and finally intense burning as that old cast iron pot caught his hand between it and the flames from the stove's burners. He yanked his hand in both pain and to grab for his sister, but his hand was trapped and the intense burning overwhelmed his senses.

CHAPTER 5

In the confessional, the priest asked, "So, what happened next?"

The old man said, "I turned and I ran. I ran away that morning, *Padre*, afraid of the demon that I had unleashed. I was so afraid of that monster, that I ran. I wanted to be as far away from her as I possibly could; and I ran.

"I have been running ever since. But it seems that no matter how far I run or how far I go, she always finds me — in one form or another. She searches for me and I know, I know that she wants to take over and drive me again."

"Where did you go?" the priest asked.

"For a few weeks, I hid in a nearby town. I stayed with the family of a friend. Miguel was one of the *braceros* who worked the fields with us. He knew what I had done (everyone did) but he also knew that I had been severely provoked by Mariana's and Jesús's betrayal. He understood that I had not been myself, that a monster had invaded my soul on that night. He was happy to help me to exorcise that demon."

"You hid?"

"Yes, *Padre*, and then began my next sin. I broke the Eighth Commandment, then, and have been breaking it ever since. I lied. The lies that I have told since those days so long ago to anyone and everyone are far too numerous to count and to tell, but there were many; some small and some large."

"Tell me about them."

"I have lied to everyone I have met since that day. I lied to my employer. I lied to my employees. I lied to government officials. I lied to my friends. I lied to my children. I lied to my wife. I have even lied to the Church, and to you, *Padre*."

He paused for a moment considering, then continued so softly that the priest had to strain to hear. "I guess that by extension, I lied to God."

Then he paused for what seemed an eternity as he remembered his flight.

Hector looked down at the coarse black hairs that lined the porcelain of the bathroom sink, then up into the mirror at the strange face that returned his stare. The dark tresses that once had crowned his head now rested in the sink below. The mustache and beard that he had sported since he first had been old enough to grow them no longer adorned his face. He did not recognize the stranger that looked back at him from the mirror (a mirror whose silver backing was peeling and leaving dark shapes in its contours). Running his hand over his head, he felt the bumps from the small cuts that the razor had made here and there across his scalp and noted how oddly shaped it was.

The top of his scalp, where once that hair had been, was a lighter hue than the rest making his head appear two-toned. He could clearly see the jawline that also was a lighter mocha color. Hector knew that he would need some sun to tan these features if he were to look as if he had been bald for any length of time.

He spat blood into the sink, the blood that came from the hole at the front of his mouth that once had housed a tooth. That tooth, he had removed to further his own metamorphosis. He looked back into the mirror and smiled to reveal the missing incisor.

Hector reached down and picked up the straight razor once again. He pulled its blade across his right eyebrow causing it to bleed from the incision. He wiped the blood and used a styptic pencil to apply the astringent that would stop the flow. He hoped that the loss of the brow and the cut would leave a scar across it that might complete his disguise.

Looking into the mirror, Hector nodded at the sight. He noted his eyes were bloodshot from way too much tequila the night before, but he did not care about that. The bloodshot eyes only aided in his disguise. Coupled with the loss of hair, beard and tooth, he hardly recognized himself. Hopefully, this was enough. Hopefully, this disguise would enable him to make a clean get-away.

He went about the business of cleaning up the mess in the bathroom and changed into the clean set of clothing that Miguel had left for him — an olive-green pair of chinos and a Glen plaid pullover with three-button placket and button down collar. Together with the fiesta hat (complete with an all wool felt body and synthetic sweatband in a cream color) his costume was complete.

There was nothing left for him to do now, but to wait for Miguel to return. As he waited he looked at the papers that the *coyote* had given him. What little information the goldenrod paper contained was typewritten. It included his basic information: height, weight, hair and eye color as well as his true date of birth.

But the name, well the name was different. The papers identified him as coming from Columbus, New Mexico and on the bottom of the little piece of paper, he signed his new name.

In the confessional, the man who had once been Hector said to the priest, "Miguel kept me informed about what had happened with Jesús and his family. He told me about the sheriffs that were searching for me. He helped me to cut my hair and change my appearance so that I would not be spotted in a crowd. And Miguel had a *coyote* friend who was happy to make false papers so that I might have a new name and a new life; one where the monster might not be able to find me. With that new name, I became the man that you know. No longer was I known by the name that had been my birthright. Hector Rivera slipped away and Alejandro Melendez was born."

Perhaps more to himself than to the priest, Alejandro, the old man who had once been Hector, whispered, "I suppose therein lies the birth of that sin."

"Continue," the priest said.

"I fled to Midland."

Later that evening, the newly named Alejandro ("Alex, to my friends," he practiced saying) drove with Miguel across the Arizona desert and into New Mexico. They spoke about his future.

"I talked to my friend in Midland and everything is arranged," Miguel said. "There is a job waiting for you. He knows that your papers are from the *coyote*, but that's all he knows - and, he doesn't want to know anything else. All he wants to know is that you are Alejandro Melendez; that you have experience working with your hands, and that you will do a good job on the rigs. He doesn't care about anything else and he doesn't want to know."

"*Yo intiendo*," Hector/Alejandro responded a bit tersely.

"Relax," Miguel replied. "It's all good. Manuel is a good friend. He understands the circumstances."

"What do you mean? You didn't tell him about . . ."

"No, no, no. No way, man. I didn't say anything about that. I just told him that you were a friend who needed work. He gets work for *mojados* all of the time. He don't care none. If he asks about a wife and family, tell him you don't have any."

"It seems wrong to deny Mariana."

"Who cares? That *puta* deserved what she got."

Holding his hand in the air to stifle the protest that was sure to come, Miguel continued, "Sorry, sorry, I know that she was your wife, and I probably should not have called her a whore, but she was cheating on you! And with that *pinche cabrón*, Jesús."

"I never knew why you hated Jesús so much."

"Don't you hate him? After what he did?"

"Yes, I hate him. But, I used to think of him as *mi hermano*."

Miguel harrumphed. "I would hate to have him as *my* brother."

"Why do you hate him so much?"

"Besides the fact that he steals from my baskets?"

"He what?"

"He steals from my basket. That's enough to hate him."

"Yeah, but . . ."

"Remember *mi hermana*, Luisa?"

Alejandro was puzzled by the question, "The one that went back to Mexico?"

"Yes, that one. Do you know why she went back?"

"I thought it was because your sister was homesick."

"That's what we told everyone. But the truth is that *ella estaba embarazada.*"

"No!"

"Yes. That *pendejo* seduced her and got her pregnant. I would have killed him right then and there if I had the *cojones* to do so. I didn't. But you did and at least you tried. Good for you. I only wish that I had."

"I didn't know."

"Nobody does. We couldn't let that kind of dishonor become known to everybody. So, we didn't tell. If I had killed Jesús then, everybody would have figured it out. So, I did nothing."

"I never knew."

"And, now, you do."

"Still, I am sorry about what I did."

"You shouldn't be. Mariana deserved what she got. I only wish you had finished off Jesús, *también.*"

"But his children, Luciana and Junior, they didn't deserve what happened to them."

Miguel shrugged and said, "They were in the wrong place at the wrong time. There was no way you could have known. Sure, I am sorry that they got hurt . . ." and, Alejandro winced at the comment, "But it's not like you meant to hurt them. You meant to take out Jesús. He sure didn't care about anyone else — including his own children — when he and Mariana were sneaking around, did he?"

"Have you heard anything about them, Luciana and Junior?"

"Luciana is still in the hospital. She is going to be there for some time. They say that she won't walk again, but who knows?"

"What have I done?" Alejandro moaned plaintively.

"It's not your fault. It's Jesús's fault. He started all of this."

"But I shouldn't have . . ."

"You did what any man would have done to protect his honor. Without honor, a man has nothing. *Mira*, look it's sad what happened to her, but you can't beat yourself up about it. It was an accident."

"Accident? I meant to kill Jesús."

"*Exactamente*. You did not mean to shoot Luciana. That was a mistake, but it was not done on purpose. Don't beat yourself up over it. You are going to have to find a way to leave that all behind you."

"What about Junior?"

"After his hand was caught in the fire, his fingers were all messed up. They couldn't save them. He lost those fingers."

"*Dios mio.*"

"He'll be fine. He is young. He'll figure it out."

Alejandro looked over to Miguel incredulously. "But I have ruined his life!"

"No. You did not ruin his life."

"But . . ."

"Hector . . . I mean Alejandro," and Miguel looked at his friend with a sly smile, ". . . *no llores por la leche derramada*. The milk is spilled and it is what it is. There is nothing that can be done about it now. Now, we have to make sure that you don't get caught by *la policia* and that you can move on with your life. Mariana got what she deserved, and Jesús will get his, too. The rest, well, shit happens, you know. You shouldn't get into trouble or have your life ruined because of it. You," and Miguel punctuated the word with a point of his finger at the other man's chest, "don't deserve that."

Alejandro's eyes began to well with tears, but he steeled himself against their onslaught. He could not let Miguel see his turmoil. Miguel would think him weak, and that would not do at all.

"You will get on with your life," Miguel continued. "You will move on. Hector is gone. Today, and from now on, you are Alejandro and someday, 'Hector' and all of this, will be a memory."

CHAPTER 6

In the confessional, Alejandro said to the priest, "I knew that Miguel hated Jesús, but I had no idea why. It was not until the night we drove through New Mexico that I learned of the things that Jesús had done. It was not until that night that I learned how truly evil my friend was."

"What do you mean?"

"Miguel told me about the many times that Jesús stole from him. He told me that Jesús often sneaked parts of Miguel's harvest from his basket and put what he had taken into his own. When caught, he denied it or blamed it on his children. I had no idea that Jesús had been doing these things. Jesús never told me about them. But neither did Miguel, or anyone else. They all knew that we were friends and, well, I guess that they thought I would not believe them."

"Stealing is wrong, that is true," the priest responded. "But that Miguel said he did these things does not make it so. Did you ever seek Jesús's side of that story?"

"Of course not, *Padre*. I only learned of them that night. There was no way that I could ask Jesús about them then even if I wanted to. It was far too late for that. I was already on the run and in hiding.

"But I believe what Miguel told me. He was not lying. He hated Jesús, but he hated him because of these things. He would not lie about the reason behind his hatred for the man. I believed Miguel then, and I believe him today. Looking back at that time, there were always the little signs; those signs that I did not see, or maybe, I just refused to see. But they were there. And looking back at them today, I can put two and two together to come up with four. Miguel was not lying. Jesús was a thief with no soul.

"And it was not only his stealing that made him a bad man. Not by a long shot. Jesús always tried to get one woman or another into bed with him. He didn't care if they were married or not. He didn't care anything about them at all. For him, they were merely new notches to put on his belt. This, I already knew about him. But I did not know how much of this was going on. I did not know that he had gotten Miguel's sister pregnant. And she was only sixteen years old at the time! Jesús should have known better than that. He should not have touched that girl. I had no idea that happened. It was not until Miguel told me about it on the drive."

"Can you be certain that what Miguel said about his sister is true?"

"I believe it, *Padre*. I know what Jesús did with other women. I know what he did with my own wife. It is not too hard to believe that he was capable of doing this too."

Alejandro nodded his head up and down — perhaps, trying to convince himself of the veracity of the claim — as he said in a softer voice, "Oh, yes. I believe."

Alejandro's mind wandered back to that day he had seen Jesús and Luisa down by the pond.

Hector (the man who later would become Alejandro, but who was still known as Hector on this day) was tying Fabia's belongings to the top of the 1951 Chevrolet Styleline DeLuxe Station Wagon. The car was ten years old, but not so old that it did not run with a little spit and prayer. Together with Jesús's 1950 Chevrolet pickup truck and Hector's own 1955 Ford F250, the two families formed part of the small caravan that would go from this farm to the McNally ranch some fifty miles away. They were expected at that ranch today so that they could begin the harvest in the early morning. Now that they had finally completed the work at this farm, it was time to move on.

Fabia put down the baby and walked over to Hector. "*Gracias*," she said to him. "I don't know where Jesús has run off to."

"I am sure that he'll be back soon," Hector responded.

"He better be," Fabia replied. "We should have been on the road an hour ago. Señor McNally is going to be angry if we do not get there soon. This is so like him. He is always doing this; never ready when it's time. We are always waiting on him, day and night, all the time."

"It will be fine," Hector said and he flashed that wide grin of his; the one that he knew always calmed her. "He probably is down by the outhouse. I will go check."

"That would be good, and tell him to hurry up. We don't have all day," Fabia responded.

Hector adjusted his hat and turned toward the trail that led to the outhouse.

These services were in another clearing, some fifty yards away from the field and the bunkhouse that housed the *braceros* during harvest season. To get to them, one walked down the trail. To the North, stood trees that formed a break between them and the fields. Hector was more than half-way to the outhouse when he saw Jesús come out of the trees on the south side of the trail. Just beyond the trees on that side, there was a small pond that often was used by the workers to clean themselves after a sweaty day in the fields or to get water for their laundry.

"What is Jesús doing down there?" Hector wondered. "He better not be swimming when the rest of us are packing up to go; *pinche . . .*"

Hector called out, "Jesús! What are you doing? What's taking so long, *pendejo*? We got to go."

"Gimme a minute. I will be right there," Jesús responded climbing the small embankment to the trail.

"What were you doing down there?" Hector asked.

"I was chasing a turkey" the other man responded. "I thought it might do for dinner tonight."

"Are you out of food, already?" Hector asked.

"No; just looking for a change. I am tired of Fabia's beans and rice."

Hector let out a little laugh at that comment.

Rustling in the brush to his left caught his attention and he started to turn toward that sound when Jesús put his arm around him and gently turned him back, away from the noise and toward where the *braceros* were gathering for the drive to the next ranch.

Hector turned and looked at his friend, "Well, come on. Fabia is asking for you and we are all ready to go. Mariana is itching to get on the road."

Nodding his head in assent, Jesús responded, "Can't keep the women waiting," then he let out another laugh.

Hector could not help but smile at his friend's infectious laughter. "*Es verdad*," he replied with a grin. "But we do need to hurry. We don't want to get there too late and find out that McNally already has enough hands for his field when we get there."

"*Vaminos*; let's go."

As they turned back toward the larger clearing, Hector heard more rustling in the trees behind him and turned to see what it was. In that brush, he saw a round face framed in long dark hair; a face that sat atop the body of a sixteen-year-old girl wearing a cotton dress. He thought, "Why is Luisa out here?" He started to ask his friend, but Jesús interrupted him with questions about the route that they would take to the McNally Ranch and Hector responded. By the time that they had reached the clearing, he had forgotten all about Luisa in the brush.

Alejandro continued his confession, "Even so, that does not excuse my own actions. I lied when I got those papers from the *coyote*. Changing my name and identity was one huge lie that I have continued for the last thirty years. It is a lie that forms the basis of my breaking of the Eighth Commandment. But it was not the only lie that I told, *Padre*."

"What other lies have you told, Alejandro?"

The old man winced at the sound of his name.

"*Padre*, if this is to be my true confession, perhaps we should call me Hector."

The priest nodded behind the grate and said, "Continue."

"It is a long drive from Arizona to Texas. It took us about ten hours driving through the night. As we drove, I continued to listen to Miguel, agreeing with everything he had to say about Jesús — even when I knew that his observations were not true. I knew that Miguel hated Jesús and I used his hatred toward my friend for my own benefit. I allowed Miguel to believe that I agreed with everything that he was saying — even when I did not."

"Why didn't you correct him?"

"I needed him. I needed his help. Because I needed that help, I did not want to say anything that might contradict him. In that way, I lied to Miguel. Perhaps it was not a very big lie and, maybe, it wasn't even a real lie at all — at least not in the sense that I said things to him that were not true. No," and he continued while shaking his head, "This was a lie of omission. It was the lie I told when I did not stand up and say that he was wrong."

"Because . . ."

"Because, *Padre* . . . because I was using Miguel; only with his help would I be able to escape what I had done. And even knowing that I was using him; that I was using his hatred to help me; I still did it. I did it even though I knew what I was doing. I did it because I had no other choice.

"But that's not exactly true, now is it? There is always a choice. Even as I sit here confessing my sins, I am lying. I am lying to you as I have lied to myself. For so many years, I have told these lies that, sometimes, I do not know the difference between truth and fiction.

"But then I wonder, if I am lying to myself unable to tell the difference is that a sin? Are the lies that we tell ourselves as bad as the ones that we tell to others? Is it a lie if we believe it?"

The priest took off his glasses and rubbed his eyes in thought before putting them back on saying, "Lies are insidious little demons. They burrow into a man and take root. When they do, they continue to grow like weeds. And, like the weeds they are, eventually, they overtake the garden."

"Yes," the man who once was Hector, then Alejandro, and now Hector again, replied nodding his head in agreement. "Yes. They do. And once they have overtaken they are almost impossible to remove.

"And so, I continued to lie. Not only about my name or who I was; but about where I came from; about my family; about every other aspect of my life. And I kept on lying to everyone. I kept on lying even after I got to Midland."

CHAPTER 7

"Hey," Daniel called out to the bartender with a raised arm and one finger in the air making a small arc meant to encompass their table, "another round."

The bartender nodded his assent and bent down to pull four bottles of beer from the cooler under the counter.

Daniel turned back to the conversation around the table.

"I don't know," Johnny was saying. "We will see what happens. Everyone was surprised to see the drop in prices last month. We were all expecting the price per barrel to go up once the US invaded, but it didn't — at least not yet."

"Do you think it will go up or down, now?" Tommy asked.

"Who knows? That shit is all fixed by the politicians in Washington and their rich friends, anyway. Don't matter none what they tell you, the truth is the rich men out there decide what's going to happen long before it does and there ain't nothing we can do about it except keep working. The rich get rich and the poor get poorer."

"Do you think there's a chance we might lose our jobs?"

"Nope. Who gives a fuck about So-Damn Hussein. So what if he went to Koo-wayt? I ain't saying it to be racist or nuthin', but what do we care about what one group of towel-heads does to another? The only thing it will do to us is make oil more expensive and that should keep us in plenty of biscuits and gravy. Why are we sending our boys over there to die for them?"

Junior awoke from his inner thoughts at this comment and interrupted, "There ain't enough oil in Texas to fuel the whole world. We need that Arab oil to keep flowing. Remember '73? When they cut us off?"

"That was a lifetime ago; almost twenty years — it was 'cause of the fucking politicians, too," Johnny insisted.

Daniel interrupted, "Any truth to the rumor that the old man is gonna sell to PermaCo?"

"Shit," Johnny replied. "Who cares? Won't make no difference no-how."

"But will there be layoffs if he does?" Tommy asked. Of course, this question was foremost in his mind. He was the new guy, after all, and if layoffs happened, he was sure to be the first to go.

"Nah," Junior replied. "The suits will clap each other on the backs and talk about how they are going to cut costs by cutting labor — meaning some of us — but the only people that will git gone are the ones in the office. The bottom line is, whether the old man still has his company or if we are sold off to someone else, they are still gonna need the pipelines, the rigs, and all that shit we make here. They're still gonna need the mules to make it. And, we are the mules."

"True, dat, Brother," Johnny said raising his beer in a toast.

"Here's to us *burros*," Daniel said raising his glass to join Johnny's.

"How long have you worked for the old man?" Tommy asked.

"Been workin' here for pert near ten years now," Johnny replied.

"Three years," Daniel responded.

"Not long," Junior said. "Just over a year."

"How long you been working the pipes?" Tommy asked Junior.

"Most of my life," Junior responded. "Used to work the fields when I was a kid. That part of the story was no joke and we were poor. But I left the fields a lifetime ago."

Junior's mind wandered back to that night so many years before when he ran from the fields and left the harvest behind.

Junior lie on his stomach in the pile of bedding that sat on the dirt floor trying not to put any pressure on the bluish-purple welts that crisscrossed the scars from older lashings. With his head tucked into the crook of his elbow, he fought back the tears that threatened to erupt from his eyes. But these were not tears of pain. These were tears of frustration and anger — an anger that bordered on rage.

Earlier that day, he had worked as hard as he possibly could to harvest the cotton that waited in the fields. When he took his bag to the weigh-master, he had gathered only one-hundred pounds. Everyone knew that a boy his size and age should be able to harvest two-hundred-and-fifty pounds during a day, but there was no way that Junior was going to meet that goal; not with his one hand that had only two fingers. He could not harvest as much or as quickly as he once could and his failure to meet his quota frustrated Papa Jesús to no end. With increasing regularity, his father lashed him with the leather belt — across his buttocks and his back. His father told him that if he were properly motivated, he would overcome his disability and be able to contribute as much as any other his age should be able.

Junior continued to seethe. What did Papa Jesús expect? It was not his fault that he now had only those two fingers. It was not his fault that his sister, Luciana, lie in a hospital bed some twenty miles away unable to move her legs. It was not his fault that Hector had come into their house that morning shooting. Did his father think that beating him would suddenly make him more able-bodied? Didn't the old man understand that the pain in his back coupled with the missing fingers only made the harvest that much harder to complete?

Besides, deep down, Junior knew the beatings had little to do with the quota. No, these lashings were borne upon the wings of guilt that his father felt over the affair that led up to the morning of the shooting. They also served as a warning that Junior should keep that knowledge to himself.

Nobody knew the genesis of Hector's rampage (nobody, that is, except for Papa Jesús and Junior). The beatings he received from his father were meant to remind him that nobody else could ever know. Even if the purpose of the lashings were not so explicitly expressed and instead masked behind the pretense of Junior's failure to meet the harvesting quota, Junior understood the real reason behind them — a warning to keep his mouth shut. Since that knowledge might lead to more inquiries from the police who had repeatedly come around these last few months seeking answers as to why Hector had seemingly gone off of the deep end, Papa Jesús felt a need to continually send Junior that reminder.

Moving slowly, Junior reached back with his good hand and

gingerly felt along the newly rising welts. He winced at the pain that shot from his buttock and up his back when he pressed on the injury.

From the other room where his parents slept, Junior heard the deep snores of his father in slumber; sounds that were heightened by the tequila he had consumed earlier this evening. That his father slept so soundly and peacefully after all that had happened only incensed the boy more and, from within, he felt his anger rise.

For a brief moment, Junior thought that his fury would overwhelm him. A heat rose within him that burned. It burned almost as much as the charring of the cast iron that licked and finally ate his fingers. That searing urged him to rise from his bedding and retrieve his nemesis — the old leather belt that Papa Jesús wielded with such alacrity. It whispered into his ear that he should take that evil tool and turn its fury onto Papa Jesús; and that he should do this now, tonight, while the old man was drunk and passed out and unable to fight back. After all, Papa Jesús deserved a beating, not Junior. Maybe if just once his father felt the lash of the leather strap he might come to understand that it was not the motivator he thought it to be.

Slowly Junior rose from his place on the floor intent upon obeying the whispers of his fury. But when, finally, he stood completely upright, a sudden need to urinate overtook him, and the whispers were silenced. For a moment, clarity of mind returned. What good would lashing out at his father produce? Would visiting the torment upon the old man, the very same torment that Junior so often endured, resolve any of his problems? In all likelihood, it would only make matters worse and the next beating would be that much more severe.

As he shuffled to the doorway, he passed his leather nemesis and resisted the urge to pick it up. Instead, he opened the door and walked outside. Although the whispers of fury had subsided, the rage within still burned. Yet, Junior resisted and he wondered whether the call of nature was divine intervention. Was his need to urinate Providence's way of silencing the demonic whispers that urged him to do wrong?

He walked down the trail that led to the outhouse and answered nature's call. When he was done, he returned to the trail headed back to his home. About a third of the way, he saw the small campfire and the three *braceros* that, even at this late hour, were passing the bottle of tequila among them.

Junior recognized all three but knew only one of them by name; the one called Rodrigo. The other two he had long ago given nicknames; Pelón and Panzón; Baldy and Pot-Belly. Their conversation drifted to his ears and he heard the name "Hector" in the winds that carried them. Quietly, he stole behind a tree to watch and listen.

"*Todos piensan que Héctor regresó a México, pero eso no es cierto,*" Rodrigo said to his companions.

"If he didn't go to Mexico, where did he go?" asked Pelón.

"Odessa," Rodrigo replied.

"Odessa?" Panzón asked with surprise. "*¿Por qué Odessa?*"

"Either Odessa or Midland; I am not sure really. Somebody was helping him to get a job there."

"What kind of job is he going to get there?" asked Panzón.

Pelón interrupted, "I heard that he was a mechanical engineer; that he went to college but he couldn't find a job in Mexico so he came here. But all that he could get was this job. The *gringos* here think he's just another *mojado*. They think that if his schooling wasn't here, it's not worth nothing. That's why he and Mariana were working the fields. Still, there is oil in Texas and Hector thinks that he can do something with his fancy education there."

"*Buena suerte para él,*" Rodrigo wished him luck. "The *gringos* ain't gonna let him have that kind of job. Like every other *mojado* around here, he will be working in the fields. Whether he is picking something on the ranch or digging for oil — he'll still be with us in the fields." The three men laughed at this observation.

"Still . . . I can't help but think about what he did to Mariana. She only had half of a face!" said Pelón.

"*Al carajo con esa perra*. She got what she deserved; disrespecting a man's honor like that," Rodrigo replied.

"What about Jesús?"

"Him, too. He should know better than to do his friend that way."

"Yeah, but the *niños. . .*"

"Collateral damage," Rodrigo said repeating the phrase he had heard on the news to reference innocents killed in the war over in Vietnam. "Sometimes, shit happens and the innocent get hurt."

"How is he gonna work in Texas with the police looking for him?" Panzón interrupted.

"You know Miguel, right? He hooked him up with a *coyote* friend. Got him some new papers."

"Do you think *la policia* will get him?"

"Nah. Miguel's friend is pretty good. Ain't heard nobody that he set up ever got caught. As long as nobody here says nothing." He looked at his companions pointedly.

As Junior listened in to the conversation, he felt the simmering rage within begin to boil. These men knew! They knew what Hector had done and they did not care! Whether Mariana and Jesús deserved what happened to them did not matter. Luciana did not deserve to be forever trapped in bed, and he, Junior, did not deserve to have his hand forever marked. Even knowing all of this, these men acted as if it had been no big deal. A woman was dead and two children (three if you count the bullet that could have killed baby Gus) were hurt. These men knew where Hector was, yet they had told nobody! They spoke of honor, but they had none. What about justice? Where was the justice in all of this?

Junior stepped back and when the sound of the breaking twig filled the quiet night, the three *braceros* looked at him as one.

"Junior," Rodrigo called out. "What are you doing over there?"

The men looked to each other as if silently asking how much the boy had overheard, and whether he would say anything to anyone. He motioned Junior over and said, "*Vente para acá*, talk to us."

"We got teeeeeequiiiiiila," said Panzón in a sing-song voice as he waved the bottle above his head to lure Junior to the fire.

Junior turned and ran. He ran as fast as he could back to his family's shack and, once inside, barricaded the door with the back of a chair. He did not know what these men might do to him now that he had overheard, but he knew that they would try to keep him from saying anything — especially to the police. He knew they would be fearful of what those officials would do to them for withholding information about Hector's whereabouts. Hector was a murderer after all. That these men might be implicated in Hector's actions would likely make them desperate enough to do whatever they felt they must to ensure that Junior did not talk. What those actions might encompass was anyone's guess, but likely would entail far more than the loss of three fingers.

For the next couple of hours, he sat in the shack looking out through the window waiting for these men to come for him. While he waited, he considered what he should do.

Papa Jesús would not want him to say anything about what he had done with Mariana. If he spilled those beans, the fire of his father's anger might consume him in much the way that the fire of the stove under the spilled beans had consumed his hand. Would he be able to endure the beating that he knew would follow?

The three men that he overheard would not want him to go to *la policia*. They would be fearful of being arrested themselves or, worse yet, deported back to Mexico. What might they do to him to keep him from talking? He knew that they would come for him — if not tonight, then on another. Would he be able to overcome that accident?

By the time the moon began to sink into the western sky and before the sun lit up the East, Junior had decided on his course of action. He would run; no more beatings from Papa Jesús; no waiting around in fear that these men might come for him. He grabbed the canvas bag, the one that he used to carry the harvest from the fields, and into that bag he packed a change of clothing.

Junior looked around the room, but there was nothing else for him to take, nothing, that is, except for the leather belt that hung by the door. This, he packed into his bag. Whether he did so thinking it might afford him some protection from what was to come or to spare his siblings that whip's wrath, he was uncertain, but take it, he would.

He stood outside the threshold of the shack, looking back within.

He looked to the table where the family gathered for their meals and saw the ghost-image of his mother serving food to Papa Jesús.

His gaze was drawn to the stove where the apparition of Luciana stood stirring that pot of beans, the one that, even on this night sat atop the stove's burners; the same old pot that had trapped his fingers, the fingers he no longer had. He hated that pot, and was not sad to say goodbye to it.

Before he closed the door on his old life, he looked once again around the walls, then, glancing from one face to the next, he mouthed a silent goodbye to each of his siblings until he came to Angelina. He stopped himself, caught by the sight of that stupid, little doll.

"*Adiós*," he whispered to his younger sister, and, then, with a rueful smile, to the doll.

Junior turned and stole into the night.

He walked down the lonely back roads until early in the morning when traffic began to pass him. Finally, around six a.m., he was able to hitch a ride with a farmer who was headed into town. The drive was long and quiet and Junior noticed that the farmer kept looking to his hand. He could tell the man wanted to ask, but was too polite to do so. When, finally, he arrived at the facility where Luciana was recovering, he shook the farmer's hand with his own, and silently thanked God that the man had not asked.

In her room, Junior waited for his sister to wake. It had been weeks since last he visited. He wanted, no needed, to explain to her. He could not simply run away without ensuring that she understood why and exacting a promise that they would remain in contact. He had to let her know that, although he was leaving, he would still be there watching over her. He would remain her protector as best as he could no matter how far away he may be.

For what seemed an eternity, Junior sat in the chair next to her bed and watched her. The sight of her slumber encouraged him until he noted that, even in her sleep, she made no motions. From time to time, her head and shoulders twitched, but there was only stillness below her neck.

Even at his age, Junior knew that people rarely traveled to the Land of Nod without movement. For so many nights, he slept (or attempted to sleep) on the dirt-floor of their home next to a passel of other children who were in almost constant motion; rolling this way, then that; kicking covers off, then alternately pulling them back; moving or twitching to the visions in their dreams. Whatever they did in their sleep, it was rare, indeed, for one to do so without movement.

Luciana appeared lost in another world. Although, she did not move, Junior heard the whispers from her lips; whispers that might have been screams within the confines of her nightmares. Who knew what monsters visited her within the boundaries of her mind? Who knew whether those monsters would ever escape?

Junior let out a heavy sigh; a sigh that emanated from the sadness that had burrowed its way deep within. As he sighed, the sadness turned to a heat; a heat that first warmed, then itched, and, finally, began to burn; a burning that did not dissipate until Luciana woke.

But when she did, it was not to favor him with the expected smile or pleasure at his visit.

"*¡Quítate de aquí!*" she whispered hoarsely and turned her eyes away from him.

"Luciana," he replied. "*Necesito hablar contigo*; I need to talk to you."

"Just go away," she said more adamantly. "*No quiero hablar*," then repeated in English, "I don't want to talk."

"But . . ."

"*¡Quítate!*" she yelled. "Just go away and leave me alone!"

"Why was she acting this way?" he wondered. She had never yelled at him before; even when they fought over, whatever it is that children fight over. This was not like her. It was not like her at all.

"Luciana," he replied. "*Por favor . . .*"

"Go away," she yelled, then averted her eyes and turned her head toward the wall.

He could not leave without explaining. He had to tell her that he was leaving. He had to tell her about his plans, but in her eyes, he saw an anger and despair that he never thought he would see in her.

The heat in his belly, again, began to rise.

"*¡Quítate!*" she yelled at him, again, and again until finally, fearful that she might rouse the attention of the doctors and nurses that were beginning to arrive for the morning shift, he acquiesced to her demand.

From the door of her room, he turned and felt the tear that slid down his cheek. The heat of that tear burned his face as the fury within him burned inside. That fury stirred and whispered to him:

"Hector did this," it said. "Look at what he has done. Look at the pain that he has brought. This is all Hector's fault. He has broken your sister."

At that moment, Junior knew what he had to do. He knew where he had to go. The trail led to Odessa. That is where the Devil now lived. He would go to Odessa and put an end to that monster. He would not return, nor speak with his sister again until he had accomplished that goal.

Deep within, the fury silenced and Junior felt a small twinge of satisfaction emanate from those depths.

"*Te quiero*," he managed to say before he turned and walked away.

CHAPTER 8

"When did you leave the fields?" Tommy asked interrupting Junior's reveries.

He was fascinated by the story. Tommy knew nothing of the hard life of the migrant worker. He had been born to white, working-class parents who had their own hard-scrabble existence, to be sure, but nothing like the stories that he had heard of the people who crossed over from Mexico. He wanted to know more.

"Sixty-something-or-other; I left the fields and never looked back."

"Must have been a rough existence."

"Back then, I didn't know any better. It just was. Looking back on it today, well, now, I know. But a child doesn't know how bad it is until someone tells him that it is, or until he has grown up and seen more of life. Then he can look back at his younger days and realize what it was. The child only knows what he knows; only knows what is real and true in his own life. It takes a lot of living to look back and understand. But along with that living and understanding comes a new appreciation for things. Sure, we were poor. Sure, life was rough. But it wasn't all bad."

Junior paused a moment, then continued wistfully, "There was good times and there was bad times. I just didn't know how bad the bad ones were until one day, then I knew that I couldn't take any more."

"What do you mean?"

"We had quotas we had to meet in the harvest. We got paid by how much we picked — the total weight. Didn't matter how many fucking hours you put in that shithole field. It only mattered how much you brought in at the end of the day. The boss weighed the harvest and gave us a slip of paper that said how much we would get paid. My papa gathered up the slips from all of us kids and every week he took them to the boss who paid him out in cash."

"Didn't you get to keep your own?"

"Hell no!" Junior scoffed at the thought. "All that money went to my papa and he decided what we was gonna spend it on. More often than not he spent it on the tequila that went down his throat."

Tommy looked down at his own beer and wondered about that. Was he spending his earnings on his own thirst? Junior noted Tommy's glance and interrupted the new guy's thoughts.

"Don't really matter what a man spends his money on. It's his own hard-earned cash, after all, and he's got a right to spend it however he sees fit. But when the man has a family, well, that's another story, isn't it?"

Feeling uncomfortable with the current topic, Tommy changed it by asking, "You been working in oil ever since?"

"Nah. When I left the fields, I moved on to other things. Doing odd jobs or whatever to make ends meet. I was still a kid, though, so it wasn't easy finding any work."

Junior looked up and caught the eye of the bartender and signaled for another round.

"How old were you?"

"Oh, I don't know, fifteen maybe. It wasn't too long after the accident that made me lose my fingers."

"What really happened to your hand?"

"I was just in the wrong place at the wrong time. Got caught up in the cross-fire of some shooting."

Tommy looked at Junior aghast. Was this true or was this just another story?

"But after that, well, let's just say my papa wasn't too happy with me. It was either leave or wait for him to kill me."

Again, Tommy was not sure what to make of this. Was he being serious, or was this the start of another bad joke?

Junior took a swig of his beer, then said, "Truth is, after the accident, I ran away. My papa was hard on me and he used to beat me if I didn't pick enough. One night I decided I wasn't gonna take it anymore. So, I left."

"You just up and left? I mean, you ran away?" The thought of a boy on the streets alone startled him.

"Yep. A couple of months later and a state or two further, I took a job at a garage."

"How did you manage to do that? I mean a kid without a home getting a job like that?"

"I lucked out. I met a real nice couple that took me in. The old man owned a garage and he gave me a job there in exchange for room and board."

Junior's thoughts wandered back to the day he met his benefactors.

Junior jumped into the filthy, brown dumpster that stood behind the old brick building just off of the town's main square. As he did so, he saw the fat man across the alley watching him and immediately thought that the man must have weighed at least three-hundred pounds. The man was dressed in green coveralls with a little red-on-white name embroidered just above the left-side pocket, but from this distance, Junior could not read the name. The fat man held a bag of rubbish in his hands and seemed surprised to see the boy duck into that squalid bin. As he closed the lid to the dumpster, Junior shook his head and placed his index finger against his lips. He pleaded with his eyes, begging the man not to give him away.

The two policemen that had been chasing him for the last hour rounded the corner and almost barreled into the fat man.

"Did you see a boy run through here?" the taller one asked.

"I just now stepped out," the old man replied.

"He's a little Mexican boy; about yay tall," the shorter cop held his hand in the air about to the level of his bulbous nose. "Black hair."

"Like I said, I just stepped out to take out the trash," the old man responded and moved toward the dumpster. "Why y'all looking for him? What he do?"

The fat man opened the lid of the bin and spied Junior crouched in the far corner, eyes wide as he watched the fat man above. The stench within the bin wafted out causing the policemen each to take a step back. Inside, Junior looked piqued

— as if the odor would make him retch, and he swallowed back his bile.

"That's none of your concern," the shorter cop said waving his hand in front of his nose as if that might deter the smell.

The fat man paused and looked at the shorter cop, then nonchalantly tossed the bag of refuse into the dumpster before closing the lid.

"Well, I ain't seen nobody," the fat man replied. From a rusted-out hole on the side of the dumpster, Junior continued to watch and listen to the men talking.

"If you see him," the taller cop responded, "you be sure to call and let us know."

"Is he some sort of dangerous criminal? This child you are chasing?" the old man asked rather sarcastically. Had he not been so afraid, Junior would have grinned at the thought of being described as a 'dangerous criminal.'

"Did we say he was a child?" the shorter officer retorted.

"Well, you did say a 'boy', right?"

The short policeman looked up at the big man with narrowed eyes, but before he could respond, the taller cop said, "Look . . ."

"Folks, 'round here just call me Eldon," the fat man said pointing to the name on his left breast. "Says it right there, 'Eldon'."

"People around here have been complaining that things have gone missing and they reported seeing this boy running around. We just want to find and talk to him."

"Hmmm . . ." the fat man nodded his head. "Yeah, I got some things been missing, too."

The shorter policeman pulled out a pad and pen and asked, "What's been stolen?"

Ignoring the shorter officer, the fat man continued to speak to the taller one. "Ain't been nothing worth making a fuss over; a couple of wrenches and some cans of oil. Might well be that I misplaced them myself. But I ain't seen nobody come down here. You might wanna check the alley across the way, though. They got some bums sleep out there at night sometimes. Might be the boy is out that way."

"Thank you, Mr. . . . . Eldon. If you see the boy, let us know."

"Sure, enough, officer. Will do."

The two policemen started back the way they came and the fat man, Eldon, looked at the dumpster before he shuffled to the open door of his shop. At the door, he watched the shorter policeman look back and he threw the cop a slight wave with his right hand then entered the doorway.

Junior continued to peer through the rusted hole. A few minutes later he saw Eldon exit the back of the building then look up and down the alley before he walked over to the dumpster and lifted its lid.

"It's alright now, boy," he said looking down at Junior. "They gone now."

Junior slowly poked his head above the edge of the dumpster and looked down the street to confirm the fat man's statement before he crawled out of the bin.

Eldon looked at the boy. His clothes were tattered, his hair was matted and he stank to high-heaven and back. After a short appraisal looking the boy up and down, with a wrinkle of his nose, he said, "You look hungry. When's the last time you ate?"

Junior did not reply.

"My wife is always making far more than a man can eat. I got some inside if you want." He turned back toward the door of his shop.

Junior stood rooted to his spot watching the fat man warily until Eldon stopped and looked back over his shoulder at the waiting boy.

"Well, c'mon now. If you want something to eat, you best get to hurrying on in here before those policemen come back."

Junior scampered behind the man into the open doorway. He looked around at the back of the auto garage as the door closed behind him. In this back area, he could not see the auto bays. This part of the shop was a small office. To the right was a large desk that brimmed over with paper. On the other side of the room, under a stairwell that led to a second floor, stood a water cooler near a table and an old Frigidaire.

Eldon moved over to the Frigidaire and opened its door, removing from within a brown paper sack. He set the bag on the table and pulled some water from the cooler in a little paper cup. This he placed next to the paper bag before taking a seat across the table and motioning for Junior to sit in the other chair.

"Go ahead," Eldon said. "Have a sit. There's a sandwich in that there bag. Hope you like egg salad. That's what my Emma made me this morning."

Junior sat down and slowly opened the bag. He noticed Eldon's eyes move down his arm to his left hand, the one that was missing the three middle fingers. Junior hid that hand under the table and with his good one removed the sandwich wrapped in wax paper. As he began to unravel the paper, his mouth salivated at the smell. He started quickly gulping the sandwich down.

"Hey, hey, there," Eldon said watching him, "slow down, now. You keep eating like that you are likely gonna choke." He pushed the cup over to the boy. "Take a sip between bites."

Junior reached over and picked up the water for a quick sip before returning to devour his sandwich. Eldon reached behind him and opened the Frigidaire again, this time taking out an apple and putting it on the table next to Junior's sandwich.

"What's your name?" Eldon asked.

Junior looked up at the big man, then between bites said, "Junior."

"Junior?" Eldon replied. "What's your daddy's name?"

The boy looked up warily at the man, then, "Jesús."

"So, you are Jeezus, Jr., then I take it," intentionally mispro-nouncing the name, anglicizing Jesús with an English "J" sound as opposed to the Spanish "H".

The boy only looked up at the man.

"Where are you and your folks staying?"

"I am alone."

"By yourself? Ain't you kinda young to be out and about on your own?"

Junior shrugged in reply, "I'm old enough."

"Where are your folks?"

"Arizona."

The man's eyes widened in surprise. "That's a ways from El Paso. What brings you to these parts?"

Junior shrugged again and said, "Parents didn't want me."

"Harrumph," the man grunted and looked down at the malformed hand. "How long you been out this way?"

Junior shrugged again, "A couple of months, I guess. I am headed to Odessa."

"Got family in Odessa?"

"Nope. Just looking for work," Junior said laconically mirroring the other man's mannerisms.

The fat man looked down at the boy for a moment as if in thought, then nodded his head before asking, "What kind of work you lookin' for?"

"I hear they got some work in the oil fields out there. Anything that I can do with my hands."

Again, Eldon looked at the boy's misshapen hand and Junior again quickly pulled it back and hid it in his lap away from the piercing eyes of the older man. Then Junior looked up and stared directly into the big man's eyes challenging him to say something about it.

Instead, Eldon asked, "How you plan on gettin' there?"

Junior shrugged again.

"Don't just shrug, boy," Eldon said sounding a tad irritated, "use your words. Cain't you communicate?"

Junior looked back at the man and said, "Walk. Hitchhike. However I need to. I'll figure it out."

"Might be easier to take a bus, dontcha think?"

"Ain't got no money." Junior picked up the apple with his good hand and took a bite.

"Hmmm," the fat man nodded, "When you plannin' on headin' out?"

Junior started to shrug, then quickly stopped himself and said, "Soon as I can, I guess."

Eldon continued to nod his head while scratching the side of his neck. To Junior, the man appeared to be lost in thought considering . . . something.

Above the office from the top of the stairs, Junior heard a door open and he started up as if to run, before he heard a woman's voice call down.

"Eldon, you 'bout done there?" the voice asked.

"In a minute, Emma," the fat man called up to the woman. "I'm talking to someone."

"Who you talking to?" the voice called back. "The shop's done been closed for pert near an hour." Junior heard the footsteps start to descend those stairs as he sat watching the fat man.

"It's alright," the man said. "That's the missus, Emma."

Junior silently listened to the woman's mutterings over the sound of the heavy footsteps she made coming down the stairs.

"The doctor done tole you that you ain't supposed to be working so damn much. You wanna have another heart attack?" he heard the woman's voice call out.

"Dammit, woman. Would you mind your own business and stop naggin' on me," Eldon called back up the stairs, then to Junior he said, "That woman's gonna be the death of me long before this ticker goes out."

"You are my 'business' you old fool," the woman retorted, and

Junior looked up at the big man sitting next to him. He could not help but grin at the man as he rolled his eyes.

Emma appeared at the bottom of the stairs and stopped. She looked Junior up and down before she said, "Well, then; who have we got here? What's your name, young man?"

Eldon responded for him, "Jesús."

"Jeezus?" Emma responded. "As in our Lord and Savior?"

"Ayup," Eldon said.

"Junior," the boy interrupted.

"What are you doing keeping my husband from coming on home? Don't you know we're closed?"

"Now, Emma," Eldon interrupted, "let the boy be. It wasn't his fault. I asked him to come in. He was hungry."

"So, did you feed him?" she asked her husband.

Junior interrupted, "Yes, ma'am. He gave me a sandwich."

"A sandwich? Good God-Almighty, that ain't no dinner for our Lord and Savior," the woman said and looked over at her husband. In the pointed exchange of glances, it seemed an entire conversation occurred between them; one that took place only in their minds; a place where Junior could not hear.

"The boy's fine," Eldon replied.

To Junior he said, "Alright, then. There's a room in the back over there," he pointed to the door that led to the garage bay, "just around the corner. Ain't much, but it's got a cot and some blankets and a wershroom connected to it." Junior noted the peculiar pronunciation of the word "washroom".

"Why don't you clean up a bit and stay there tonight before you head on out?"

"I don't think . . . I probably should just go now."

"Ain't no trouble at all. You will be safer back there than you would be out on the streets tonight. Besides you stink to high-heaven and back. You need a bath. Ain't gonna get no work smelling like that. Once you're cleaned up and rested a bit, you can do what you want. It's still a free country."

The big man got up and pushed his chair back behind him. "Don't make no difference to me," he continued. "Do what you want. But if you are here in the morning, I'm sure Emma would send down a fine breakfast to fuel your journey."

"Of course," Emma responded. "We got manners. Ain't no heathens in this house and we always make room for a wayward stranger — especially if he's our Lord and Savior."

"Thank you," was all that Junior could think to say to this strange couple.

"Alright, then. G'night." With that the big man took his wife's elbow and led her up the stairs and out of the garage.

Junior looked after the man's departing form and thought to himself, "What an odd couple. What kind of a man would let a total stranger sleep at his place knowing nothing about the stranger?"

But he was tired. And it was true that he needed a bath. So, he made his way to the "wershroom" and cleaned himself. He was somewhat bemused as he looked to the cot thinking on the fat man's words. "*Ain't much*," he had said, and Junior let out a tiny laugh as he looked around. Sure, the room was small, but not any smaller than the ones he usually slept in. It was also true that the cot wasn't at all very large, but it was a couple of feet off of the floor — a floor that was covered in linoleum. Accustomed to sleeping on a dirt-floor atop a pile of blankets, the cot seemed quite luxurious to him.

Junior fell into that cot and covered himself with the blankets. He could hear the muffled conversation that was going on in the rooms above the garage, but not clearly enough to make anything out. He considered stealing up the stairs to listen in, but he was so tired that he was almost asleep before his head hit the pillow. His last thought was "a pillow."

Junior was sweeping the floor of the garage when Eldon came down the stairs that next morning.

"Morning, Savior," Eldon said.

"Morning," Junior replied with a wry look on his face. He wasn't sure if he liked being referred to in that manner.

"Put that down," Eldon responded. "Emma done sent some breakfast over for you. You wanna eat it before it gets too cold."

The big man walked back to the little office and set down the covered plate of food that his wife had sent with him to give to the boy this morning. He looked down at the plate as if thinking that he would not mind having some more of the biscuits that were housed underneath the cover. He scratched at his big belly, then with a heavy sigh turned to the coffee maker.

"*Gracias*," Junior replied and placed the broom at the doorway before he sat at the table to eat the food that the older man had brought.

"Don't say grassy-ass," the old man responded intentionally mispronouncing the Spanish word. "I don't mind that here, but if you wanna make something of yourself, you best be speaking English." Eldon poured a steaming cup of coffee for himself, then sat at the table next to the boy.

Junior only looked up at the man, then nodded.

"How'd you sleep?" the big man asked.

"Fine," Junior replied between bites of eggs, bacon, and biscuits and gravy.

"Well, you certainly smell a lot better. I guess the wershroom was good enough?"

"Yes, sir."

"How's the food?"

"*Muy bueno* — very good," Junior said.

"Yeah. If there is one thing that crazy, old bat upstairs is good for, it's for her way 'bout the kitchen." Eldon patted his large belly as if to emphasize how much he enjoyed his wife's cooking.

Junior grinned and continued to eat his breakfast as Eldon watched him seemingly lost in thought.

"Well, now listen," the big man said when Junior was almost done. "Me and Emma done had ourselves a little talk last night. Seems that we gave you some dinner yesterday and some breakfast this morning. I gave you a place to stay last night, and now I'm gonna ask you to do something for me in return."

Junior hesitated and looked up at the man warily. "Of course," he thought, "the old man wants something. Nobody ever does anything out of simple kindness. That's just the way of the world." Even at his young age, he had figured this out.

"What do you want?" Junior asked.

"That old bat upstairs may flap her gums a lot, but she ain't wrong about one thing. The doctor did tell me to slow it down. See, I had a heart attack a few months back; probably on account of my being heavy," and he patted his belly to emphasize. "He told me to lose some pounds and to take it easy. But I cain't take it easy, you see. We got lots of folks depending on us 'round here and lots of work to get done."

"Ok," Junior said, not sure where the fat man was going with this little speech.

"I need some help 'round this here garage 'cause I can't keep doing it all on my own. The job don't pay much, just a little walking-around money, but it comes with room and board. You can sleep in the back room over there as long as you keep working and Emma will make you three squares a day."

Junior was taken aback, not at all certain how to respond. "I don't . . ." he started, but the big man held up his hand to interrupt him and continued talking.

"I know. I know. You got someplace you think you need to be. But you ain't gotta be there right-away do you? And you done said that you ain't got no money. It's a long walk from here to Odessa and people on the roads might not be as kind to a young boy . . ."

"I ain't no boy," Junior interrupted.

". . . to a young *man*," Eldon continued now emphasizing the last word. "Even if that young *man* is our Lord and Savior."

Again, Junior bristled at the description, but said nothing.

"Besides, you might recall, if you read your Bible, that people weren't always so nice to that first Lord and Savior, either. You would be a lot better off if you earned a little bit of money so you could take a bus, don't you think?"

Junior only looked at the man trying to figure him out; what a strange creature he was.

"You would be doing me a might big favor if you stuck around awhile and helped out 'round here. More importantly, you'd be helping me get the old woman off my back."

"Well . . ."

"Besides, you owe me. At least for last night. This here way, you get to pay me back for that and shut up the old bat to boot."

Junior looked at the big man. He knew that Eldon did not really need his help. He knew that the man and his wife would be just fine without him. He knew that Eldon's offer was only a way to turn the big man's charity into something that Junior felt he had earned. But knowing all of this did not detract from the truth. He could use the money. He could use some rest. He could use some food in his belly. It had been a long, hard past few months. Maybe sticking around for a little bit would not be the worst thing in the world. Besides, the room, the cot, everything about this place was so much nicer than what he was used to. Staying here would almost be like staying in the *gringo's* Big House back at the ranch.

"Ok," he replied. "I can stick around for a couple of weeks, but then I have to go."

"Understood. Now go on to the back. You will find some coveralls that should fit you. Old man Rosenblatt is bringing in his wife's Caddy here shortly and we are gonna have to do an oil change."

Junior stood to retrieve and don the coveralls. Before he could walk away, Eldon said, "Hey now, take them there dishes on over to the sink. You cain't be leaving that mess around unless you wanna feel the wrath of the old woman. Ain't no reason both of us should be on the business end of her tongue-lashing. She'll come down and get 'em later."

Junior did as he was told. That afternoon, Eldon taught him how to change the oil in "old man Rosenblatt's" car. Later, he taught him so much more about working on these vehicles.

Those weeks turned into months, and those months into years.

CHAPTER 9

In the confessional, Hector said to the priest, "For the first five years, I drank almost every night. I guess that is another sin . . . the sin of gluttony. Does that fall under the Ninth Commandment, *Padre*; 'Thou shalt not covet'? Is gluttony a form of covetousness? If it is, is it truly a sin if the transgression was not from desire but from fear? I didn't drink because I liked the bottle. I drank to forget.

"Each night I was visited by the ghosts of my past. They came in nightmares that included Mariana or Jesús's children, Luciana and Junior. I drank to keep them at bay. And, sometimes, the haunting was not from the memories of what I had done. No, sometimes, those visits were from *La Furia* herself. That demon was continually trying to possess me once again. It was only at the bottom of the bottle that I was able to fight off her advances.

"Every night and every day I drank myself to oblivion. When I was drunk, I passed out and did not have the dreams that otherwise came."

To his ward, the priest replied, "I have known you for years, Alejandro, and never once have I seen you drink."

"Please, *Padre*, my real name is Hector. Let's finally dispense with that lie."

"The man I know as Alejandro does not drink."

"Ah, but Hector did," he said as he considered his time in Midland.

Before his arrival, Hector Rivera died and Alejandro Melendez was born. But, Alejandro was not born a child, rather he was born a thirty-five-year-old man; the progeny of fear, desperation, and the services of the *coyote*.

For the first five years of this decade, Alejandro worked the oil fields that once had been thriving, but were now mere shadows of their former selves much like the man, Hector, that Alejandro had replaced.

Midland, so-named because it was the mid-railway post between Fort Worth and El Paso, was founded in 1881. At that time, cattle shipping was its largest business. But in the 1920s, oil was discovered in the Permian Basin and Midland began to boom.

Like much of the country, and even the world, the Great Depression took a heavy toll on the city. But in 1943, the Spraberry Trend was discovered. This oil field is one of the largest in Texas covering some 2,500 square miles in parts of at least six counties. The end of World War II brought with it an influx of veterans seeking work, and development of the basin spurred an economic boom in the area. Even through the troubling times of foreign oil import expansion in the 1960s, the field drew investors and speculators.

Although Alejandro was not a young man, neither was he old. He was in those middle years of his life — that time when a man usually has made peace with himself and found his footing — but not so with Alejandro.

These last years of his life had not been easy. First, there had been the fretful flight from the ranch near Springerville, Arizona. That flight that had left him breathless and trepidatious; afraid of the monster he knew was still out there, and fearful of the long arm of the law that he worried might yet reach out for him. He found employment in the oil fields of Midland and, in the ensuing months and years, he kept his head down and lived his life as best he could, comporting with the accepted standards of society; never veering too far from the straight-and-narrow road — or so it seemed to those around him. He worked hard and paid his taxes. He was the model citizen. If there was one thing in which those among him might find fault it was in the copious amount of spirits he so often imbibed.

Those who heard Alejandro cry out in the night might say that he drank to forget his past. How could they know that Alejandro Melendez, in fact, had no past? Those long-gone days belonged to another man, the one named Hector. Can a man forget a past that he never had?

Others considered that Alejandro drank to forget the trials and tribulations of his present circumstances. They mused that he used alcohol as medication to soothe a tortured soul — even if they did not know what tortures he endured. But if a man's present is no more than the sum of his past, what is that present to a man who has no past?

Still others opined that Alejandro drank out of fear of a future that was yet to be written; a future that none could see.

When asked directly, Alejandro only said that he drank to ease the regret he felt; a regret for the what-might-have-been. On that point, he elaborated no more. In time, those around him stopped asking and accepted him for the man that he was — a man with a proverbial monkey on his back. More often than not, the roughnecks with whom he worked found themselves carrying him back to the bunkhouse when, in the wee morning hours, the lights in the bar announced its closure.

When he thought about it, Alejandro understood that he drank to stop the dreams — those nightmares that came so often whenever he lay his head down to rest. He drank to block out those nights; those nights when Mariana visited him wearing the same housecoat and old pair of *chanclas* she always wore — the pink slippers with the little blue rose sewn into the top. She came to him on these nights wearing the same beautiful smile she wore on their wedding day; a smile that always melted his heart. But then like his heart, her smile melted, and her eyes which once had looked at him adoringly stared at him in accusation. On those nights, he looked into those eyes and her once beautiful face until that face disappeared into a blanket of crimson.

He drank to block out those nights when the girl, Luciana, found him in his slumber. She crawled into bed next to him and whispered into his ear. On those nights, he strained to listen, but could not hear what she spoke. It was not until she motioned with her hand that he looked down her torso. Each time that he did so, he discovered that where once there had been legs, now, there was nothing. Then the whispers became screams, "*¿Por que*? Why did you do this? Why did you take my legs?" Those screams continued until he woke in a film of sweat.

He drank to stop the visits from the boy, Junior, who crept to the side of his bed and thrust his hand in front of Alejandro's eyes.

The boy said not a word, but forced the man who once was Hector to stare at the hand which ended only in knuckles where the three middle fingers should have been. Junior made him look at that hand that now sported the mark of *La Furia*.

He drank to block out the nights when the visage of *La Furia* appeared trying again to lay claim to his body. On those nights, he fought and thrashed against her insistent demands; thrashing about to compel her to cease her attempts at dominion of his soul. This continued only until he woke from the fit.

He drank because late at night, passed out in an alcohol-induced stupor, Alejandro had no such dreams. He drank; not to forget the past or to soothe the present. Nor did he drink for fear of his future. He drank to obliterate the dreams.

What difference did the constant chittering of the monkey make? When the monkey whispered in his ear, "Go ahead, take another drink," it was not his adversary, but his ally. That monkey may be insistent, but the monkey preserved his sanity, or so he felt. Under the influence of the monkey, the dreams did not avail. And for the first five years of his new life, he obeyed that monkey.

"What finally caused you to stop drinking?" Alejandro's confessor inquired.

"The love of a good woman. But that took some time. Before that, I drank and continued to work. But I grew tired of working for another man. I yearned to find my way on my own."

"What did you do?"

"In or around 1973, together with my friend, David, we purchased some two-hundred acres out in the Basin. The plan was simple.

Each of us put up an equal share of the money to buy the land and, of course, the mineral rights. We started drilling. We moved from spot to spot hoping to strike a field, but never seemingly able to. But there was a lot of land and we knew that it was out there if only we could find it. It was a long process and we worked each and every day, seven days a week.

"I guess, that is when I broke the Third Commandment — failing to keep the Sabbath a day of rest. I drove myself to utter exhaustion as we kept searching."

"That is a sin, but not one that cannot be forgiven," the priest responded.

"But that was not the only Commandment broken at that time. We were running out of money. Unlike me, David had a family to feed and although we continued to work for the big companies to bring in extra income, it was not enough. So, we broke the Seventh Commandment, 'Thou shalt not steal.'"

"What did you do?"

"As I said, we were still working other jobs and working ourselves to the bone moving from site to site on our own land. Our equipment was old and faulty. We did not have the money to purchase new. So, we began to take from our employers. It started off small, stealing only little items to repair what was worn out on our own. Still, it was not enough. While I was able to get another loan to continue our search, David was not.

"We were on our fifth or sixth well when David came to me wanting to give up. But I knew, *Padre*, I knew that if we kept at it, we would strike oil. I couldn't give up on the dream so easily. "

"What did you do?"

Alejandro thought to that morning in the diner.

Alejandro looked at the man sitting across the booth.

"So, what do you think?" he asked.

"I am not sure that I understand all of the legal talk" David replied. "What does it all mean?"

"Essentially, I am giving you a loan to cover your share of the expenses."

"What about this 12% interest rate? I never did understand interest," he said wondering about the rate. Didn't he hear somewhere that at this time, the interest rates hovered between eight and ten percent?

"In order for the bank to make money on giving you a loan, they charge interest on the loan. That's how they make their money."

"I get that, but why am I paying *you* interest?"

"Because I am taking out the loan. The bank is charging me interest. So, this paper says that you will pay me back for the money that I put out and the interest that you pay to me is to cover the interest that the bank is charging me, so that when you pay me back, you are also paying the interest that I am going to have to pay to the bank."

David pushed aside his empty breakfast plate and continued to read through the legal papers in front of him and asked, "What is all of this about mineral rights?"

"There are two parts to all of this. One is the land itself and the other is the mineral rights. In order to get the new loan, the bank wants both to be put up as collateral."

"So, why do I have to give you my mineral rights?"

"The bank won't give me the loan without them. It's the rights that are valuable as collateral. The land itself is not really worth all that much."

"Two hundred acres ain't worth much?" David asked incredulously.

"Not two hundred acres out here where nothing grows. That land has no value except for its potential. That hinges on whether there is oil underneath."

"I still don't understand. Why do I have to sign all of the rights to you?"

"Because the bank won't give me the loan on only some of the rights. They want all of the rights put up as collateral. Without that, there is no loan. And since you cannot qualify for the loan, only I can get it. So, to get it, I have to have all of the rights."

"But I will get them back?"

"Of course; of course," Alejandro replied with a wave of his hand. "Once the loan is paid off, the bank won't care who has the rights in their name and we can revert your share back to you."

"That makes sense, I guess."

"It's just the way that it is done."

"Well, I never understood all of this legal gobbledygook."

"It's just how banks work."

"I guess you would know Mr. Fancy-Pants-College-Man," and he laughed at this descriptive.

Then, Alejandro shrugged and said, "So, what do you think?"

"Well," David considered, "I guess, if it's the only way that we are going to be able to do this, then that's what we are going to have to do."

He took the pen and signed his name at the bottom of the page.

"I convinced David to sign over all of the mineral rights to me. I needed them in order to secure another loan."

"And your friend agreed?"

"Of course, he agreed. He was not very smart and he did not understand all of the ins and outs of the land and rights purchase. He didn't really understand any of it at all. Sure, he knew the mechanics of getting oil out of the ground — and that is what I needed him for — but the rest, well, the rest was lost on him. Unlike me, David had only a high school education whereas I had a college degree. He trusted me to make the right decision. He trusted me to be true and fair.

"How could he know that trust was misplaced? How could he know that the interest rate I charged him was well above the interest rates at the time?

"Usury is a sin, this I know, *Padre*, but under which Commandment does it fall? I am not at all certain. Regardless, we can add that to my growing list."

The priest nodded on his side of the confessional taking a mental note.

"What happened, next?" the priest queried.

"What I knew always would. We struck pay dirt and we had a celebration that night."

Raising his glass in a toast, Alejandro said, "Here's to all of our hard work. And, here's to the money that we are going to make!"

David joined Alejandro in his toast clinking their glasses together. Each man at the table wore a wide grin that stretched across his face and each believed that no matter what happened on this night, his grin would never fade.

For the last few years, they had worked the oil fields of another man, until the day that they determined to venture out on their own.

By hook and crook, bargain and theft, they obtained the necessary equipment to drill and search in the hopes that the land might spout forth black gold. For months, they labored, but today, finally, their sweat and tears bore fruit.

"So, what do we do next?" David asked Alejandro.

"Tomorrow, we look for someone who might be interested in a mineral lease for two or three years."

"How much do we get paid?"

"Usually, there is a signing bonus, but after that, we get a royalty."

"What does that mean 'a royalty'?"

"A royalty is our percentage."

"So, what does that mean in terms of money?"

"Well, we got two hundred acres out there. Let's say one well for every fifty acres; that's about four wells. If each well draws one hundred barrels a day — and I am just estimating to make the math easy — if we get one hundred barrels per day out of each of those wells that's four times one hundred or four hundred barrels per day. Oil's going for $15 a barrel, so that's $6,000 per day. If we get a twenty percent royalty that's $1,200 a day — about $440,000 a year, give or take."

David whistled through his teeth and, even though he thought that it wasn't possible, his grin widened even more. "That's two hundred grand each."

"Well, there are a lot of if's in there, but yeah. And, of course, that doesn't consider taxes and all that."

"Is twenty percent normal?"

"We'll ask for more, but I think we can get fifteen to twenty after we negotiate."

David let out a loud whooping sound and they continued to drink the rest of the evening.

CHAPTER 10

"I need something to eat," Johnny said interrupting the conversation. To Daniel he said, "Pass me that menu. Dinner's on me, girls."

Nobody knew why Johnny was suddenly feeling uncharacteristically generous, but none were going to pass on the opportunity to have him pay for their meal.

"I shouldn't," Junior said. "Ginny is sure to have something waiting for me when I get home."

"Just have a little something. Don't have to be a full meal," Johnny replied as he handed the menu to Daniel.

Daniel opened the menu and looked down its contents. Not that there was much to see. This was not really a restaurant after all, it was a bar. But they did have some light snacks and pub food available.

"I will take a burger," Tommy said.

"Come on, Junior, just a little something," Johnny asked.

"Nah, I will just eat some fries off of Tommy's plate," Junior replied.

"The hell you will," Tommy responded with a grin and laugh.

"They got tacos?" Daniel asked.

"Do you see tacos on the menu?" Johnny responded.

Daniel looked back down at the menu and squinted his eyes. "How about flautas?"

"You gotta order off the menu. This ain't some fancy place where they will make whatever you want."

"How about cheese sticks?"

"Read the damn menu."

"I am just thinking . . ."

"Are you slow or somethin'?" Johnny interrupted and tapped the top of the menu impatiently. "Look at the damn menu."

Daniel looked back down and squinted at the words. They were not mere squiggly lines with no meaning. He knew what they were and even what they represented. He recognized them as letters of the Roman alphabet, but the various combinations made no sense. To him, these letters were no more than jumbled marks on a page. Whatever meaning they held in these specific combinations was lost on him, and that was his secret shame. For so many years he had been able to fake it. Nobody knew or understood the extent of his illiteracy, but hours passed in the tiniest of moments as the other men at the table watched him stare down at this cypher. He felt a heat rise in his face as it flushed red in fear that his shame might finally be exposed.

Seeing this Junior quickly discerned the issue. "Hey, Daniel," he said. "I ain't all that hungry. Wanna share some nachos with me?"

When Daniel looked up into Junior's eyes, he saw the awareness in them and his face reddened. But that embarrassment traveled with relief. Thank God Junior had made the offer. Perhaps he could hide his shame a little longer.

"Yeah," Daniel replied and carelessly tossed the menu aside. "That sounds good."

"Alrighty, then," Johnny stood. "I will let the bartender know."

Tommy stood, "I gotta hit the head."

"Thanks," the other two men said in unison as Johnny walked away.

"*Gracias*," Daniel said to Junior after the other men had left the table.

"*De nada*," Junior replied. "I know how it is. For a long time, I couldn't read. Still don't read so good now, but that couple I told you about earlier, the woman, she taught me."

"It's hard," Daniel said.

"You can do it. Just need practice. Practice makes perfect."

Junior smiled at the memory of Emma saying the exact same thing so long ago.

"Dee-tur-mined that . . ."

"Determined," Emma corrected the boy.

Junior took in a deep breath and started again, ". . . Determined that thruff . . ."

"Through," the old woman, again, corrected.

"That don't make no damn . . ." Junior retorted.

"Language," the old woman warned lifting her index finger as she did so.

"Sorry, but it don't make sense. Earlier you said that e-n-o-u-g-h was 'enuf', but now you say that t-h-r-o-u-g-h is 'through'. They are the same!"

"The English language has all sorts of variables like that. 'Cough' ends in o-u-g-h and is pronounced like 'off' while 'through' which also ends in o-u-g-h is pronounced with the 'oo' sound. And there are other ones, like 'bough' . . ."

"What's bow?"

"It's where a baby sleeps. It's spelled with an o-u-g-h and is pronounced like 'ow'."

"English is dumb! How is anyone supposed to learn to read when the same letters put together are pronounced so differently?"

"That's just the way the language is. I don't know why. I didn't make it up. It just is. And you just gotta learn 'em. I have spent many-a-year down at the church helping children to read — and not just children, but others like you, people who maybe knew some Spanish, but needed a helpin' hand to get by in an English-speaking land. They all ask the same questions and the answers don't change none. It is that way, because that's the way it is."

"But it's so stupid!" the boy tossed the book down as he felt his frustration level rising and with the frustration his anger.

"Hey now, there ain't no call for that."

"I am sorry. I just don't get it. Spanish makes more sense."

"That may be true, but this here ain't Spain, and it ain't Mexico, either. You gotta learn to read, write, and speak in English if you wanna make something of yourself."

"But why do I need to? I don't need to know how to read to fix a car."

"You don't?"

"No, I don't."

"You sure about that?"

"Don't need to read to figure out what part goes where."

"But what happens when you can't figure it out? What happens when you have to pull out a manual and read it to figure it out? If you can't read, you won't be able to do that, will you?"

"I'd figure it out."

"Might be that perhaps you would, but what if? Do you think old man Rosenblatt is gonna be happy if you send back his caddy to him and it ain't working because you couldn't? Think he is gonna pay you good money for fixin' something that ain't been fixed?"

"Ok. I get it. But how am I supposed to learn all these different spellings?"

"You just do. The words may be spelled similar, but they can be pronounced differently. You learn through practice. You get that practice through reading. Practice makes perfect."

Junior sighed and pulled the book back toward him. Looking down at the page he continued from where he left off, "Determined . . ." and he glanced up at Emma to get her approving nod, ". . . through the ma-gik . . ."

"Magic," Emma corrected. "Remember the 'g' can sound like a 'g' or like a 'j'."

". . . through the magic of redding . . ."

"Reading"

". . . reading, he could go into any world he wanted."

"Good! See that wasn't so hard. Now read that sentence again."

"The boy determined that through the magic of reading, he could go into any world he wanted."

"Very good!" Emma smiled down at him and Junior looked up beaming, happy to have made her proud. "Now put that book aside. We are done reading for today. We'll pick up where we left off tomorrow."

"Good."

"Here," she said handing him a sheet of paper.

"What's this?"

"That's your vocabulary list for today."

"Oh, man," Junior replied with a shake of his head and exaggerated shrugs.

"Don't you roll your eyes at me, young man," Emma responded with a shake of her head. "Vocabulary is an important part of reading."

"Why do I need to know all these words?" the boy protested.

"If you don't know what something means you are gonna forever be asking. Every time you ask me what something means in English, that's vocabulary; just like every time I ask you to tell me how to say something in Spanish. It's important if you wanna be able to talk to someone, right?"

"I guess, but. . . "

"Ain't no butts in this house."

"But I don't want to . . ."

"'Don't want to?' 'Don't want to?' Boy, there are many a day that I 'don't want to' but I do it anyway. You gotta do what you gotta do no matter the 'don't want to.' Life is what happens when you 'don't want to'. But I guess if 'Our Lord and Savior' 'don't want to' . . ."

"Why do you keep calling me that?"

"What? 'Our Lord and Savior'?"

"Yeah. I ain't nobody's savior. I hate that."

"You hate your own name? Child, I didn't name you."

"Can we just . . ."

"Just what? Do what we 'don't want to'?"

"Why do I gotta do this today?"

"What's wrong with today?"

"Nothing. It's, well, it's just not fair! This ain't how it should be!"

The old woman looked over to the boy seated in front of her, took a deep breath, then said, "Child, whoever tole you life was 'fair'? God don't give one whit whether life is 'fair'. It is what it is, and you best be learnin' to deal with the 'what is' if you ever wanna get to the 'what should be'.

"Who pissed in your Post Toasties this morning? Why are you in such a mood?"

"It's just today of all days,"

"What's so special about today?"

Junior paused for a moment, then blurted out, "It's my birthday."

Emma stopped short and looked at the boy. On her face, he could practically read the thoughts that whirled around her. "How did I not know?" she wondered. "Why didn't he tell me before? He has been here for nearly a year and I never thought to ask. How stupid of me!"

Junior read all of these thoughts as they danced across her face and immediately felt a heavy guilt. The last thing that he wanted to do was to make this woman feel anything but love from him. She had been so good to him and he never wanted to hurt her in any way.

Finally, Emma nodded slowly. "I see." She said. "You never told me."

"I'm sorry," Junior started, but the old woman interrupted him.

"Ain't nothing to be sorry about. Don't ever say you're sorry for something you didn't do. Sorry is for the bad things that you do and should be said only when you mean it — otherwise, it has no meaning. A 'sorry' without meaning is meaningless. Understand?"

"Yes, ma'am."

"I'm sorry that I never thought to ask."

The boy's eyes welled with tears and he angrily brushed them away.

"Now, now," Emma said and reached over to take him in her arms and hug him. "You stop that right now. Ain't no call for tears in this house. Lordy, I am so stupid. You must be missing your mama on today of all days."

Junior held the woman, hugging her back and said quietly, "You are my mother."

"Now, boy," Emma said softly. "Don't be saying that. I may love you like you was my own, but you got a mama out there and I bet she's missing you something fierce."

"I doubt that."

"Come on, now. Maybe we should reach out to her; give her a call and let her know that you are ok? Maybe you want to talk to her for a spell?"

Junior pulled back and looked the woman with steely eyes. "No," he responded as firmly and surely as he could muster.

"Ok. I get it."

"I don't want to talk to her. As far as I am concerned, you are my mother."

"Ok. Ok." Junior could see the consternation in woman's face as she pulled him back to her and held him tighter. "God knows I love you," she said. "And I guess you are old enough to make that decision on your own."

Then she let out a little laugh. "Good-God-Almighty, I am guessing you are old enough. How old are you anyway?"

Junior laughed through his tears, hesitating before he answered, "Sixteen today."

Emma sighed. "Sixteen. Well, now, that ain't so old. But I guess it's old enough. Eldon and I was married when I was still sixteen. Of course, he was a might bit older than I."

Junior pulled back from the woman's embrace and pulled his arm across his nose as he sniffled in.

"Now, don't be doing that," Emma said. She reached into her housecoat and pulled out a linen handkerchief. "Use this."

"I'm sorry," Junior said again.

"You stop that, right now," she said back. "No more sorries."

"I'm sorry," Junior repeated, then laughed as the old woman gave him a stern look and a shake of her head with a rueful smile.

Emma sighed heavily, then said, "Since today is your special day, we're gonna skip the vocabulary lesson and pick that up tomorrow." She looked over at him and said, "Now, git. Go on downstairs and help Eldon out in the garage. He's probably madder than a wet hen that I kept you up here so long. And now, well now, I got me a birthday cake to bake, don't I?"

"I don't need . . ."

"Shush, child. Everyone gets a birthday cake in this house."

Junior smiled at her, then rose from his chair and made his way down the staircase that led to the garage below.

CHAPTER 11

"If you want, I can ask Ginny to help. I know that she would be happy to."

"You would have your own wife teach me?"

"Sure. She would love to."

"I am just so *avergonzado*."

"Ain't no need to be embarrassed," Junior said.

"But you know that Johnny will never stop teasing me."

"Those *güeros* won't understand, but I do. I been there, *primo*. I get it. I won't tell."

"Do you really think that she can teach me?"

"It's not so hard once you get the hang of it. Then it just takes practice and more practice."

"It would be nice to be able to read better."

Junior looked over at Daniel and opened his mouth to speak, but at that moment, Johnny and Tommy returned to the table stifling any further conversation about illiteracy.

"Food's on its way," Tommy said and placed a beer down in front of Junior and Daniel.

"Thanks for the beer," Junior said, then to Johnny, "and for the food."

"I gotta ask," Tommy said as he took his seat next to Junior, "So, you were an auto mechanic before working the pipelines?"

"Yep," Junior took a swig from his beer. "I worked on cars for a long time in El Paso."

"That when you got that sweet ride?" Johnny asked.

"I've had that car for years, now. I am surprised the old hunk of junk is still running."

The men at the table laughed. The car was a 1964 Ford Fairlane and each and every man at the table knew how much Junior loved that car. Just as they knew how much care he put into it. When he was not working, or having a drink with his buddies from the job, he spent his days tinkering on that car. The men often joked that Junior loved the car more than he loved his wife and child.

The car was more than twenty-five years old, and that Junior had kept it in such pristine condition these many years was testament to his attachment to the vehicle. It was not that he could not afford to purchase a new one, but for some reason, he chose not to, and that reason escaped them. What they did not, or could not, understand, was why he loved it so much.

It was not as if the Fairlane was a classic car that was sought after by many auto aficionados. There was nothing particularly special about the make, model, or year. Yet, Junior had held onto that car all of this time and whenever something went wrong with the vehicle, he searched far and wide for the proper replacement parts to be certain that it remained in its original condition.

"Where did you get it?" Tommy asked.

"Oh, a long time ago, when I worked at the garage in El Paso. The old man that owned the garage taught me everything that I know about cars. Together, he and I bought it and fixed it up. It was practically brand new back then, the owner — some teenage kid — had an accident and just about totaled it. He sold it to me for scrap. We spent months working on the car. With a lot of work, we got her running. I learned a lot from that old man."

"Do you ever work on other cars?"

"Sure," Junior replied. "Gotta problem with your car?"

"No, but, hey, you never know. And if I do, I'm gonna need help."

"The newer cars are harder to work on. On some of them, you need some specialized equipment to figure out what's wrong and how to fix it up. I like these old ones. Most of the time, the problem is easy to find and fix — if you can get the parts."

"I know a little bit, but not nearly enough to keep anything running for long. Seems every car I get ends up in the junkyard."

"That's because you drive like a woman," Johnny said, and the men laughed.

"It's not that hard," Junior said. "Once you figure out what you're doin', it all falls into place. Besides, what you don't know, you can look up in a manual. The old man used to say that I had a knack for it, though."

Junior's mind wandered back to the day he got his first, his one and only, car.

"Savior!" Eldon called from downstairs.

"What?" Junior called back down. "I'm reading."

"Ain't got no time for that now. Get your ass on down here."

"But, Emma said . . ."

"I don't give a good-God-damn what that old bat said, get your ass on down here, now!"

Junior wondered what he had done. Eldon was often cranky, but in a loving way. He yelled and used foul language often (which Emma was always on him about: "Think about what you say in front of children!" she admonished) but Junior knew that the old man did not mean anything by it. But today, well, what could he possibly have done to get the old man's ire up? He closed the book, pushed it aside on the table and started down the stairs.

"Hurry your ass up, boy!" Eldon called again as Junior reached the bottom steps.

"What's going on?" Junior asked then saw it. Eldon was standing in front of a lime-green 1964 Ford Fairlane. Although, the vehicle was practically brand new, it was completely trashed.

Junior let out a long slow whistle as he looked at the smashed-in front end, the missing fender and door, large scrape down the right side, and blown out tires.

"What happened here? Is that Jacob's?" Junior asked.

"Ayup. Rosenblatt's grandkid done messed up this one damn good."

"How did he do it?"

"Stupid kid went drag racing out on Pike Road."

"Is he okay?"

"He got a few bumps and bruises, but he's fine. Likely hurtin' more from Rosenblatt's tongue-lashing than anything else. Had it been me, I would have whooped that kid good."

Junior winced, remembering the beatings from his father, then, "Sheesh," he said as he walked around the car surveying the damage. "Would you look at that!"

"Ayup. It's a might shame, too. Boy ain't got no respect for these here machines. Some people think the world owes 'em and act like it do. Kids these days ain't got no respect for nobody or nuthin'."

Shaking his head, Junior responded, "Might be better off just junking it and buying something new."

"That there's the problem," Eldon waxed philosophically. "It's like I always told you; a car ain't no toy. It's a tool; a machine; meant to make our lives easier. Too many people these days don't respect the tools they've been given — whether it's a car or somethin' else. They use 'em up and throw 'em away. Why junk this just because the person who had it don't know how to treat it? It can be fixed-up."

"It will be expensive; likely cost more than a new one altogether."

"Well, I don't think young Jacob's gonna be gettin' any new ride soon. Rosenblatt was pretty pissed off."

"I don't even know if it can be fixed."

"What you mean?" Eldon responded. "Ain't nothing that's too tore up can't be fixed with the right proper love and care."

Junior looked at the big man for a moment and thought, "Is that what you and Emma are doing? Trying to fix me with love and care?"

An immense wave of love for the other man almost overwhelmed him. But instead of saying anything so maudlin to him, Junior replied, "It will be expensive and take forever."

"Rosenblatt don't care none about the cost."

"Must be nice to have that kind of money. Is he willing to wait all the time that it's gonna take?"

"He don't much care 'bout that none now no how. Ain't like Jacob's gonna be riding around in this, or anything, anytime soon."

"'None now no how', what?" Junior asked with a mischievous grin.

"You know what I'm saying. Don't sass me, boy," Eldon said returning Junior's grin.

Over the years these two had teased and cajoled each other mercilessly, but it was all done out of great affection.

"Yeah; I can understand that. Why would Rosenblatt give Jacob another one? But this . . ." Junior shook his head thinking, ". . . this will take months to fix up."

"Ain't his problem no more."

"What do you mean?"

"You got wax in your ears, Savior? I said, it ain't his problem no more."

"Sorry," Junior said in an exaggerated voice indicating that he was anything but. "Whose problem is it, then?"

"It's your problem now, Savior."

Junior looked over at Eldon quizzically. "What do you mean?"

"You gotta fix her up. I'll give you a hand, but this here is now your responsibility."

"Ugh. Seriously? This will take forever. What about all of the other work? What about my reading?"

"The other work ain't gonna stop. You still gotta help out on anything else that comes in. This here's a special project and can take as long as it takes betwixt everything else."

"Ugh," Junior said and shrugged.

"Boy, what I tell you about shrugging?" Eldon responded.

"Sorry," Junior replied.

"I done made a list over there of everything we are gonna need — at least to start. Why don't you call around and order the parts?"

"Yes, sir," Junior responded and walked back to the office at the back of the shop as Eldon stared at his departing back. Unknown to Junior, when he entered the office, Eldon smiled a large grin, then turned to look at the wrecked vehicle. He let out a loud whistle that Junior heard from behind the walls of the office.

For the next several months, Junior worked on the Fairlane. With Eldon's guidance and occasional assistance, he slowly and arduously repaired the damage that had been done to the vehicle. He repaired what he could repair and ordered replacement parts for what he could not. He straightened the frame and replaced the door. He buffed out and filled in the scratches. He painted the car. All of this was done between the hours spent working on other customers' vehicles and his continued reading lessons.

More than once, Junior had to consult the manual and each time he did so, he had to confess to himself he was happy to have finally gotten those reading lessons.

"Emma was right," he thought and smiled.

Throughout the process, Junior learned more and more about the work involved in auto repair, and became quite adept at machinery in general. As he worked on repairing this wreck, he gained a love and appreciation for the simple complexity of the machine: how each and every part fit together just so to form a working piece that performed the service it was intended to. He came to love cars and machinery in general and garnered a special affection for this particular one.

When the months had passed and the repairs were finally complete, Junior looked down at the Fairlane with a sense of pride. He had done this all with his own two hands. He polished and caressed its fender, then called to Eldon to inspect the final product.

Eldon walked around the car, bending down, looking inside and out, checking each and every nook and cranny. Junior knew that if the car was not perfect, Eldon would make him go back and re-do whatever it was that he deemed inadequate.

When he was done, Eldon turned to Junior and said, "You did a real good job, son."

Inside, Junior beamed with pride. No sweeter words had ever been spoken to him. "In the end," he thought, "isn't that what every boy wants — the love, appreciation, and respect of a father; to know that he has made him proud?"

But all that Junior said to Eldon in response was, "Thank you."

"You test it?"

"Yes, sir. Took her out on the road this morning. Everything is running just fine."

"'Just fine'?"

"Perfectly."

"That's good. That's good," Eldon said nodding his head up and down.

"Old man Rosenblatt should be happy," Junior said.

"Ayup. Except that . . ." Junior looked up at him quizzically, ". . . I spoke to Rosenblatt yesterday. Seems Jacob got hisself into a might bit more trouble here, lately."

"What he do now?"

"The old man didn't say and I didn't ask. No need to go digging into someone else's business. He wants me to know, he'll tell me."

Junior nodded in reply.

"Seems Rosenblatt ain't all that interested in this here car no more."

"What do you mean?"

"He don't want it for hisself and he ain't gonna give it to Jacob."

"What's he wanna do?"

"I asked him that very question."

"And?"

"Well, you want a ride dontcha?"

Junior looked back at the fat man in complete incomprehension. "What? I don't understand? Speak plainly old man."

Eldon let out a big laugh as he heard his own voice coming out of the younger man's mouth. When he stopped, he looked over at Junior and said, "Happy Birthday and Merry Christmas, son."

"What do you mean?"

"It's yours. Bought it from Rosenblatt on the cheap. He didn't wanna pay for the repair, so I worked out a deal to buy it for what it was worth when he dropped it off; basically, scrap. It's yours now, son."

What Eldon did not say, what he could not say, was that he had bought that car many months back — on the very day that it had been dropped off — knowing that he intended to give this vehicle to Junior; using it to teach the boy a valuable lesson about pride in work and the boy's self-worth.

Junior's jaw dropped, then closed and dropped again. He blinked three times as understanding began to dawn on him, then closed and opened his mouth again. But no words came out. He did not know what to say.

Eldon laughed at Junior's obvious discomfort, then reached over and clapped him on the back.

"Every young man needs a project. Somethin' to keep him out of trouble. And every young man needs a car. Figured I'd kill two birds with one stone here."

A huge grin crossed Junior's face. Then, he reached over and embraced the fat man in his arms.

CHAPTER 12

"Hey," Johnny yelled out to the bartender. His bellowing interrupted Junior's thoughts. "Can't you put something else on the television? That war shit is getting boring."

From the corner of the bar, above the bartender's head, the TV had been showing non-stop coverage of the Gulf War and the so-called "shock and awe" campaign. Johnny had grown weary of the reporting.

"Yeah," another patron from down the way called out, "put on a game. We're sick of that shit."

The bartender picked up the remote and began surfing through the channels. As he moved the dial up, the face of Nancy Kulp filled the screen. The voiceover of the reporter said that the actress had passed away. This caught Junior's attention. He had loved that actress in *The Beverly Hillbillies* and she died young (only 69 years old!) of cancer. The newscaster spoke of the family's statement, then the bartender changed the channel again — looking for some sporting event or another to assuage the patrons. Junior's mind began to wander, but his thoughts were interrupted by Tommy.

"I been meaning to ask you," Tommy said between bites of his burger and gulps of his beer, "What's that tattoo about?"

"This one?" Junior looked down at his left bicep and flexed the muscle. Carefully stenciled across its expanse the word "Lord" was written. "Or this one?" He flexed his right bicep to display the word "Savior."

"Well, both. What do they mean? You never struck me as a church-going man."

Junior laughed, "Truth be told, they don't have much to do with faith. I know that together they say 'Lord' and 'Savior', but I was never a religious man."

"Then why did you get them? What do they mean?"

"It's sort of a nickname. Everybody calls me Junior, but my name is actually Jesús. In Spanish, you say 'hay-sus', but in English, it's pronounced 'jeezus'."

Tommy nodded in understanding.

"My . . . mother used to . . ."

"I thought that you ran away?"

"I did. I mean, not my real mother, but the woman who raised me after that. I called her my mother even though she really wasn't. In most ways, she was more of a mother to me than the real one."

Junior pause momentarily with a far-off look in his eyes before he continued, "Most of the time, she was a caring and loving woman, but sometimes she could be a difficult old bat. Of course, she never meant anything by it. She wasn't mean just to be mean."

Junior let out a little laugh in remembrance of Emma.

"She used to tease me about my name all of the time. It would piss me off to no end back then. She called me 'Jeezus, Our Lord and Savior.' How that used to get me worked up."

"So, the tattoos are for . . . what?"

"I got 'em for her. To honor her. She passed several years ago and I wanted to have a reminder."

"Yeah, I got this one here to remind me of my baby sister," Daniel said pointing to a little tattoo on his chest over his heart. "She died as a kid."

"As a kid?" Tommy asked. "What happened?"

"Car accident. My papa was driving us home. We had been out getting ice cream. One of those rare days when he took us out for anything. Driving home, a deer ran out. He swerved and we went off the road."

"That's horrible," Tommy replied.

"It happens," Daniel said and shrugged his shoulders. Seeing the shrug, Junior could not help but think of Eldon. "The sad part is that my momma could never forgive him. I got the tattoo when I was a teenager."

"Cool," Junior replied.

"No tattoos here," Tommy said. "Never could get up the courage to get one. Did it hurt like people say it does?"

"Not too much," Junior replied. I got them both done at the same time. 'Lord'," and he lifted his left arm to look down at the ink, "and 'Savior'," he said looking down at his right.

Johnny interrupted, "There are some good church-going folk that might not take too kindly to ya'll taking the Lord's name in vain, like that."

"I don't give a good-God-damn what people think," Junior retorted. As the words left his mouth, he heard Eldon's voice and smiled.

In response to his smile, Johnny grinned, lifted his bottle of beer in salute and said, "I'm with you there, *amigo.*"

The sound of Eldon's voice in his head coupled with the picture and story about Nancy Kulp emanating from the television in the background sent Junior away into his own thoughts once more.

Junior sat in the chair at the tattoo parlor as the artist put the final touches on the 'r' in the word 'Savior.' He looked down at his right bicep to admire the work when the artist proclaimed it finished. The fluid letters in their medieval script and dark blue ink were easily discernible even through the red puffiness of the arm.

The artist reached over and picked up a small jar of ointment. Junior was uncertain what it was, "Vaseline?" he wondered. The artist rubbed the ointment over the area of skin then bandaged the tattoo with a light film of plastic wrap.

"Keep that covered and dry for a bit," the artist said.

"Yes, sir," Junior replied.

"It's gonna scab over, but that's normal and it will heal. The scab will fall away on its own. You might feel a little burning for a couple of days, but that's normal, too."

"Thanks."

Yesterday's funeral had been the first that Junior had ever attended. After his godmother's death, his own family had not gone to her service. Even if they had, Junior would not have gone, sitting at home as he had been at the time nursing his injured hand.

Today, it was not a wounded hand that he nursed, but a wounded heart.

Pancreatic cancer, in fact, any cancer, is a diagnosis that strikes fear in most. It is the most aggressive and least treatable of all of the cancers and Emma had been diagnosed only four months prior to succumbing to the disease. Those four months had been a roller coaster for both Junior and for Eldon. Alternately, Junior was depressed, then angry, then numb; then depressed and angry all over again.

For so many days, he watched this beautiful woman, the woman who had been a surrogate mother to him — a mother that he never felt he had before she came into his life — as she slowly succumbed to the ravages of the disease.

At her bedside, he tenderly wiped her forehead and face with a damp cloth to cool her burning skin.

When she was too weak, he prepared meals for her, and, then, held the utensil whose weight was too great a burden for her to carry.

He read to her from the many books that she had given him; books meant to teach him, but now used to distract her from the tortures her body endured.

When she was ill from the so-called medicine the doctors prescribed, he held her hair as she ejected the contents of her stomach into the pool of liquid at the bottom of a porcelain bowl.

Eldon was beside himself the entire time, and unable to function at all. He would not leave his wife's side except to answer the calls of nature when those calls became too loud to ignore. He left the management of the garage to Junior, who duly obliged when he, himself, was not tending to their patient.

On the morning that Emma passed to the World Beyond, Junior sat silently at her side as Eldon slept in the chair next to the bed. Before she joined the Highwayman on his journey, Junior watched her lips as she whispered what he thought were silent prayers.

She opened her eyes and looked to the corner of the room. Junior followed her gaze, but saw nothing, then turned back to her.

He heard her say to that corner, "You cain't have him. He ain't mine, but he ain't yours either. He belongs to God."

Emma's gaze turned to Junior and she whispered, so softly that he had to lean in to hear.

"Remember," she whispered. "There ain't no monsters, except for the ones that we make."

Emma closed her eyes for the last time and Junior looked to the clock at the side of her bed. It read 6:21.

The tears that Junior stifled burned hot; hotter than any tears should. A heat burned within him and with the heat, came the return of the whispers in his head; the whispers that demanded justice for all of the indignities of his life; justice for his fingers; justice for his sister's legs; justice for his god-mother; justice for . . . well, everything and anything.

"But, what is justice? What is right?" He wondered.

Surely, this was all Hector's fault. Of course, Hector had nothing to do with Emma's death, but in Junior's mind he knew that everything, absolutely everything, that ever had happened to him since that fateful morning so many years ago was the direct and proximate result of his godfather's actions.

The whispers in his head confirmed this to him. They said that, but for Hector's shooting that morning, he would not have run away and he still would have his Mama Fabia. That he had managed to find Emma and Eldon was a testament to Junior's own resourcefulness. That he came to love Emma as a replacement for his own mother was a testament to Emma's innate ability to inspire devotion. It was Hector's fault that he had no mother.

The whispers in his head continued to indict Hector. But for Hector's shooting, Luciana would be here now to comfort him in his grief; the same comfort that she always gave to him before, when still she could walk to him and care for him. It was Hector's fault that his sister could do so no longer. It was Hector's fault that he had no sister. It was Hector's fault that he found no comfort.

The whispers in his head prosecuted his belief in Hector's guilt. But for Hector's shooting, he would need no comfort, since he would never have come to know the beautiful soul that was Emma; a soul that had now left this worldly plain.

Junior silenced the whispers momentarily considering that perhaps he should be thankful to Hector for that.

Then the whispers returned, "Thankful!" they said. "There was nothing to thank that *pendejo* for."

Everything that Junior felt, the anger the pain, all of it derived from Hector's actions, they insisted. Each and every trial and tribulation in his life emanated from that one man's actions.

The whispers grew louder.

"Justice!" they demanded. "Find Hector. Make him feel the wrath of Justice," not mere justice, no, but Justice with a capital "J".

The ultimate Justice must be meted out against his godfather; against the man who was at the root of the evils that had been set upon him; against the monster.

But when Junior's mind conjured pictures of Emma's face, he knew that it was not justice the whispers demanded, but vengeance. He heard her final words once again, *"there are no monsters, except the ones we make,"* and, when he heard her voice, he stifled the whispers in honor of her.

In the days that followed, Junior knew that this was more than he could bear. And the whispers grew louder. Each and every morning, Junior rose to the incessant whispers. Each and every morning, he turned his thoughts to Emma in the hope that she might help him to silence their calls; the calls of the rage and fury that burned within him.

CHAPTER 13

Turning to his ward, the priest asked, "But you no longer drink?"

"I stopped drinking some time after that," Alejandro responded.

"When I drank, it was to deny the false god. I drank to ward off *La Furia*, but when I stopped drinking, she stopped coming.

"Oh, she never completely ceased her relentless assaults. Even now, there are many nights that I still must fight off her advances. But after a time, I learned to do this without the aid of liquid spirits.

"That was so long ago. Perhaps, it was my new-found success along with the love of a good woman that frightened the monster away. It was the love of a woman that gave me the strength to give up that particular sin.

"Who knows what may have happened to me if I had not met my Carmen. Who knows where I would be today if it had not been for her."

"Tell me about her."

"The first time that I saw her was one evening while David and I were still trying to find oil in the fields."

It was an autumn evening and Alejandro sat on a stool next to David in their local watering hole. They had only just arrived having put in long hours trying to strike that black gold in the Texas desert. Alejandro was not yet as drunk as he surely was going to be before the end of the evening. He ordered another shot of tequila and another beer, then, after downing the shot, heard the creak of the front door as it opened. He swiveled in his stool to see who was entering. He did not do this out of any particular interest. He was not a terribly curious man. But something drew him to the sound and, for once, he looked.

She was a blonde-haired beauty with a light complexion that spoke to a life that was not spent out-of-doors; a life of ease and comfort. She had piercing green-eyes that looked inquisitively around the room. When those eyes briefly fell upon Alejandro, he felt his heart skip a beat and as she sauntered, cat-like, toward him, he could not help but stare.

When, finally, she reached the spot where Alejandro and David sat, she spoke and, although the music from the jukebox played on, the sounds that emanated from it, in fact, all other sounds in the world stopped. The only sound that Alejandro heard was the music of her voice.

"David," she said ignoring Alejandro altogether.

David turned and looked at his wife. "Carmen," he said and

reached over to peck her cheek. At that moment, Alejandro's heart dropped and he felt empty; as if he had been drained of everything. He sat on his stool and watched as the woman returned David's kiss, then David continued, "This is Alejandro. Alejandro, meet my wife, Carmen."

"Hello," she said, then flashed the most brilliant smile that Alejandro had ever seen. She extended her hand to him and for what seemed to him an eternity, he did not speak; lost as he was at the sight of her; mesmerized by this creature in front of him. He noted the shape of her chin, the nape of her neck, and the ears that were slightly too large for her head, yet somehow seemed to balance into perfection. But it was her movement that enthralled him; each motion, each step, each gesture punctuated an inner confidence that he had never seen in any woman before.

He looked down at her extended hand, and when he found his voice, Alejandro reached out and shook it. A jolt of electricity ran up the length of his arm almost knocking him over.

As he steadied himself, he responded, "Nice to meet you."

"*Con mucho gusto,*" she replied again with that smile.

Alejandro was surprised and amused to hear this white woman speak to him in his native tongue. Was she Irish or, perhaps, German? He never expected to hear Spanish pass from her lips; those beautiful, full, and ever-so-inviting lips.

With eyebrows raised, he asked, "You speak Spanish?"

"Yes. My grandfather lived in Mexico."

"You are *Mexicana*, then?"

"No. My grandfather was one of the settlers at Colonia Dublán."

"How interesting."

"Just a bunch of old family history," she replied with a flash of that brilliant smile again.

Alejandro looked back at her unable to keep himself from grinning.

Carmen turned toward her husband and said, "It's time to come home."

"We were just having a beer," David replied.

"Drinking time is over," she said. "Let's go."

David looked to Alejandro with an exaggerated grimace and then, with a shrug of his shoulders, said, "The Mistress of the House has spoken," then in *sotto voce*, "She doesn't like it when I drink." He downed his beer and rose from his stool. "See you in the morning."

As David and his wife turned and started for the door, Alejandro called to them, "It was a pleasure to meet you, Carmen." She turned back and flashed her amazing smile again before giving him a half-hearted wave on her way out.

When she exited the same door that she had entered, that moment of eternity seemed far too short. Inside, he yearned to follow her, drawn by her wake.

Alejandro heard the chittering of the monkey demand to be fed, but that chittering was drowned out by the memory of her voice.

In his mind, he heard David say, "She doesn't like it when I drink."

That was enough for him. He did not give in to the monkey's pleas. Instead, he locked that monkey into a cage. Swiveling his stool back to the bar, he asked for his tab.

Later that night, when Alejandro retired to his bed, his head was filled with thoughts of the woman. For the first time in such a very long time, his dreams were not haunted by the apparitions of his past. The ghosts of his sins did not visit and there were no demands from *La Furia*. Rather, that night's fancies were filled with visions of her.

In the morning when he woke, he wondered whether that was because he had been besotted by the drink or if he had been besotted by her.

"What happened then was but another of my many sins."

"What did you do?"

"I broke the Tenth Commandment. I coveted my partner's wife."

"Did you act upon those feelings, Alejandro?"

"Please, *Padre*, call me Hector. Alejandro is but the manifestation of another sin. He does not exist. He never did. Hector is the sinner here. It is Hector who is giving his confession."

"Hector," the priest tentatively replied, "did you act upon those feelings?"

The old man whispered, "I knew better. After all that had happened; after Mariana's affair with Jesús, I, of all people, certainly knew better."

The old man shook his head, then continued, "But I could not help myself. I was bewitched by her. It was as if everything about her was designed to lure me in. For the next several weeks, I took every opportunity to be near her. If David invited me to dinner, I accepted his invitation, even though I had never considered it before.

"Each time she was near, I was satisfied only to see her. Even if she never spoke, the mere glimpse of her was enough to satiate the growing hunger that I had to be near her. If nothing else, the sight of her was enough to save me from the nightmares that otherwise plagued my sleep."

"And?"

"I had never felt so drawn to a woman before, and I could tell that she felt the same. Oh, I had loved Mariana, but this, this was so very different. Knowing that she was in the world was enough to bring me pleasure. But knowing that she was there, yet out of my reach, was agony. Isn't it strange that a man can feel both pleasure and pain at the same time? Isn't it odd that those two opposites can exist beside each other?"

"Pleasure and pain; light and dark; good and evil; they are two sides of the same coin, Alej . . . I mean, Hector."

"Yes, indeed, they are. I found myself playing with that single coin. Flipping it in the air to find pleasure on the one side then pain on the other."

"Did you give in to temptation?"

"I knew that she wanted to. And, so did I. But it was many weeks before we gave in to our desire and once we did . . . well, to see her was pleasure, but to smell her perfume; to taste her lips; to feel the touch of her skin against mine; that was ecstasy. She completed me.

"And, so, I broke the Sixth Commandment. I committed adultery with another man's wife."

"Even after Mariana?"

"Even after Mariana. Carmen's seduction was everything. Nothing else mattered. When I was with her, everything else faded away."

The two men sat silently in the confessional; priest and sinner, as each man considered all that had been shared. When it seemed that Hector would say no more, the priest prompted, "Do you have any more to confess?"

Hector let out a little laugh. Had that not been enough? Did not his many sins already condemn him to an eternity in the flames of hell?

To the priest, he responded, "Yes, *Padre*. There is more."

"Continue, my son."

"While I searched for a company to buy the lease, I continued to see Carmen. We snuck out together whenever and wherever we could. David was drinking heavily, continuing his celebration of our great fortune, so he was rarely around, and it was not difficult to find stolen moments. But then there came the time when Carmen and I met and I noticed the bruises on her face."

"Bruises?"

"Yes. I asked Carmen about them and she told me that David had hit her."

The priest drew in a sharp intake of breath as Hector continued.

"The moment that I saw her beautiful face so bruised, I felt the fire in my belly begin to burn. I felt the rise of *La Furia*. I searched my apartment for the gun that I had hidden away. I would have killed

David that very night, but for the angel that was beside me. Carmen calmed me and exorcised *La Furia*.

"Together, we hatched a plan that would rid her of David and free us to be together. She would, of course, divorce him, and then she and I would be free to marry.

"I know that the Church considers divorce sinful, but it was not spiritual interests we pursued.

"Even so, that was not enough, *Padre*. It was not enough to steal his wife. Given that he had beaten her, we knew that we had to destroy him to ensure that he could not come after us. So, we plotted to break the Seventh Commandment."

"What did you steal?"

"Besides another man's wife? I was not content with that; oh, no. You may recall that David had signed over his mineral rights to the land. Those rights were in my sole possession and under my name only. So, on the day that I sold the lease, I sold those rights in only my name. I worked it out so that I stole any chance he had of ever getting his share of the proceeds from that oil.

"But you had promised . . ."

"Yes, I had promised him. On the day that he signed the papers for that second loan, I promised him that I would return the rights to him once we succeeded in our quest.

"It is not that I had intended to swindle my friend on that day. It is not that I had intended to steal his wife, his land, or even his money. Even if, in retrospect, I maneuvered him into signing the necessary paperwork at the diner so long before. It was simply happenstance that all worked out as it did. Some hidden hand guided me along a path that set me up so that, on this day, the very day that Carmen had him served with the divorce papers, I had taken from him everything."

"*Dios mio*," the priest replied.

"Now Carmen and I were free to be together and we had the money to do whatever we wished."

On his side of the grate, the priest shook his head.

Hector continued, "I was absolutely taken with her and barely remember the terms that were agreed to, or anything else about the day that I sold that lease. All that I can recall was how stunningly beautiful she was. It was more than I could have ever hoped for.

"Later, when the child was born, it was with only the briefest of moments that I recalled my wife, Mariana, and her inability to bear my fruit. For that tiniest of moments, I remembered who I truly was.

"But I pushed that away. Whomever Hector had been in the days before this, he was no more. I was complete. Alejandro was rich beyond his wildest expectations. Alejandro Melendez was a family man.

"Looking into the eyes of my newborn son, for an instant, I thought that I saw *La Furia* staring back at me through those eyes. But that image quickly faded and all that I saw after that were the usual eyes of a bright and beautiful boy.

"I have not had a drink since then . . . but tonight, well, tonight, I hear the calls of the monkey in a way that I have not heard in many, many years. The monkey did not call to me even after what happened to David."

"What happened to him?"

Hector's thoughts wandered back to that night.

"Carmen!"

Alejandro watched as his love shuddered at the sound of her name being shouted into the night. He walked over to the window and looked down from his third-floor apartment to the broken man who stood on the sidewalk yelling her name. David was holding a bottle of whiskey in one hand and swaying to and fro as he yelled again.

"I know you are in there! Just come out and talk to me!"

"Shut up, *boracho*," someone called out from the apartment above.

"Fuck you!" David yelled.

"I'm calling the cops," the voice from above could be heard yelling down.

"Carmen!" David called out again.

Alejandro turned away from the window and knelt beside Carmen then cradled her in his arms. "It's ok," he said. "It will be alright."

"What if he doesn't stop?" she asked.

"He's drunk. He will get tired of yelling soon."

"And if he doesn't?" she asked.

"Sooner or later, he'll just pass out," Alejandro responded and Carmen rewarded him with a flash of that smile that always melted his heart.

"I love you!" they heard from below. "Don't do this to me!"

"God, I wish that he would stop!" Carmen said.

Alejandro stood and moved to the window again. Pulling the curtain to the side so that he could peek out. He saw that David now sat on the sidewalk. As he looked down his eyes were drawn to the bottle of whiskey that David had tipped to his lips, and he felt a tingle in his throat and heard the chittering of the monkey. But he pushed away the sounds of that beast and continued to watch.

The last few weeks had been extremely stressful for him as he finalized the lease that cut David out of the profits from the oil. They had been difficult on Carmen, as well, as they went through the process of filing, serving, and then moving forward with the divorce proceedings. But even given these stressors, he had not felt the need to drink. It was not until this night as he looked down at the shattered remnants of his friend that the monkey's calls became incessant. Still, he resisted. With Carmen at his side, Alejandro felt that he could hold out against anything.

Rain began to beat against the window pane as the skies opened and droplets of water fell from the clouds above. He could not help but feel sorry for his one-time friend as he heard David swear below at the wet that started to envelop him. From down the street, he saw the lights of approaching cars and behind them, he noted that the third one back was a police cruiser. Alejandro returned his gaze to the man below and watched as the man tried to stand, then stumble back before righting himself.

"Carmen!" David yelled up to the window again.

"Shut up!" Alejandro heard from the window above.

"Fuck off!" David yelled above then threw the bottle of whiskey toward that window. It crashed and broke against the side of the building falling far short of its intended target, but the momentum of the throw knocked David off balance and he stumbled back into the street.

Alejandro heard the squeal of the brakes before he saw David fly through the air and into another vehicle coming from the opposite direction. He heard the sound of breaking glass as that car's windshield imploded. Alejandro closed his eyes and turned away from the window.

"What was that?" Carmen asked.

To the priest, Hector responded, "He died.

"I cannot help but believe that it was no accident. I think that he wanted to die that night. I think that he purposely set himself on the curb of that street with the intent of throwing himself in front of a car if he could not get Carmen's attention. And when she refused to come out, I think that he did it on purpose. I guess, there is another one of my sins. Although, I am not at all certain which Commandment encompasses that."

"If he did commit suicide, that is not your sin."

"But for our actions, mine and Carmen's, he would not have died. Surely, I bear the responsibility for that; if not in a strict sense, at least in a moral one. And is not God's law the moral law?"

"You are responsible for your own actions and your own sins — not for the actions and transgressions of others."

"But it was *my* sins, it was *my* transgressions, that lead David down that path."

"You cannot be held accountable for another."

The old man harrumphed. "Can't I? Shouldn't I? Everything that I put into motion led to what happened. Just as everything that I did so many years before led to what happened to Mariana and to what happened with Jesús's children.

"Are we not each and every one of us responsible for the events that we set into motion?"

CHAPTER 14

Tommy took a drink from his beer, then turned to Junior and asked, "So, not too much pain from getting them?"

"The tattoos? Not as much as other things," Junior replied.

In response, Johnny belched loudly to the laughter of the men around the table then interrupted with, "We all got our crosses to bear."

"Ain't that the truth," Daniel replied.

The game on the television went to commercial break and a brief news short about the continuing fighting in Kuwait momentarily caught everyone's attention. They reported that Hussein's forces had intentionally set some oil fields on fire. Simultaneously, protesters in California were marching and chanting "No War For Oil! No War For Oil!"

"Damned idiots," Johnny muttered almost under his breath.

"There ain't no surplus of smarts going 'round these days," Junior replied.

"Yeah, well, this ain't got nothing to do with oil. Why they gotta be hatin' on oil all the time?"

These were men from Texas; born and bred. These were men whose livelihood depended on the flow of that oil. For them, calls to stop that flow were nothing more than an attempt to prevent them from earning a living; to impoverish them. These were calls to stifle their way of living — indeed, to wipe out their very existence.

"It's not really the oil," Daniel responded. "They hate Bush."

"Ain't that the truth," Johnny replied. "They would be against anything he did. The man could cure cancer and they would blame him for the loss of jobs in the drug industry."

The men at the table laughed at Johnny's joke. Whether the laughter was because they truly thought the joke funny or because more and more beer was imbibed was anyone's guess.

Tommy turned to Junior and, changing the subject, asked, "Hey; why go from auto mechanic to pipeline work? Working on cars seems like steadier work — without the boom and bust of oil."

"I was pretty good at it, but I guess I wanted to do something different," Junior started to shrug his shoulders, but caught himself. That little movement returned his thoughts to Eldon.

Junior sat in the garage smoking his cigarette while reading the latest letter from his sister, Angelina. After Emma's death, he had reached out to the girl wanting information on his family. He wanted to know how they were doing. Whether this was because he felt a need for connection to this past after Emma's departure from his life, or, for some other reason, he did not know.

Turning to the letter, he read:

July, 1971

Dear Junior,

I was so happy to receive your letter and am happy to hear that you are doing well! As you have asked, I have not told anyone that we have been writing — not even my husband, Lazlo. But I have to admit that it doesn't feel right keeping things from him. Regardless, I have kept my promise to remain silent about our letters and will continue to do so until you give me permission not to.

He thought he heard a thump on the ceiling above him and paused to listen. Eldon was upstairs watching his television as he so often did these days.

Recently, the fat man (who was no longer so fat, having lost nearly a hundred pounds!) was quiet and withdrawn and not at all the man that once he had been. Prone to bouts of depression, there were long stretches of time that went on for days wherein he never came into the garage at all, instead leaving all of the work to Junior.

When he wasn't watching re-runs of *I love Lucy* or *The Andy Griffith Show*, he watched one of the myriad game shows that pervaded the airways. Although, Eldon watched these shows, Junior knew that the old man wasn't really seeing them. When he sat in front of that television set, there was always a faraway look in his eyes indicating that his mind was elsewhere.

As Junior listened for more sounds from above, he flicked on his cigarette and watched the gray ash fall into the already overflowing tray. When no further sound was forthcoming from upstairs, he returned to the letter.

Let's see; what's been happening since last we wrote? My husband, Lazlo, got a new job at the power plant. He is doing well and we just bought our first home in East Austin. It's not very far from where Mama and Papa live so it is easy for me to visit regularly. Mama appreciates that I come around and so do the younger ones that still live at home. My daughter, Rosita, is now two years old (Can you believe it? Two years old!) and is walking and talking up a storm. I wish you would come home to meet her. She is beautiful. Never in my wildest dreams did I ever think that I would have such a wonderful and caring husband and such a beautiful child.

It was hard for Junior to believe that Angelina was now a grown woman with a child of her own. In his own mind she was, and, likely, forever would be, the little girl from his memories.

Another sound emanated from above, and Junior again cocked his head to listen. He was not the least concerned that Eldon rarely worked in the garage anymore, leaving that to Junior. The boy (who was now a man) did not mind so much. He rather enjoyed the work and the interaction with the customers that streamed-in on a daily basis.

But on the other hand, he was angry with Eldon. Emma had been gone now for over two years. While Junior missed his surrogate mother intensely and understood the deep-seated loss that Eldon felt, he also knew that it was long-past time for Eldon to move on. As sad as that may be, it was true. Two-and-a-half years is far too long for a man to grieve his deceased wife.

Junior stubbed out his cigarette into the ashtray, spilling some of the spent butts across the desk. With his good hand, he swept the ashes away, then lit another cigarette and returned to his reading; letter in one hand and cigarette alternating between his other and his lips.

We have joined a church nearby. The pastor is Lazlo's brother, John. He is quite the preacher. I never thought that one day I would leave the Catholic Church for another, but Pastor John has taught me that we don't need to blindly follow the Church to be closer to God. He hears us whether we speak to Him through the Pope and his followers or if we speak to Him in our own way. In this new church, I am finally finding the peace that I could not find with Father Joe. (You remember Father Joe, right? The priest at the church not far from the ranch — the one that we used to go to every Sunday.) Pastor John is my rock and he has taught me so much. I thank God each day for bringing him to me.

Junior wondered when Angelina had become so religious. Sure, as a child, she went to church each and every Sunday; they all did. But as he thought about it, he had not gone out of any deep-seated faith in, or devotion to, God. He went because Mama Fabia made him go. He remembered sitting in the pew listening to the priest drone on and on. Mass was rather dull and boring and Junior figured that most children, if given the choice, would much rather play outside on a nice Sunday morning than sit indoors listening to a boring sermon.

Then, in his mind's eye, he saw Angelina as she was back then — a small child sitting in the pew beside him, eyes wide, enraptured by the ritual and pageantry of it all. He recalled that each night before bedtime, the little girl knelt in the corner with her hands folded in prayer. Perhaps, he would have seen her budding religious fervor had he only opened his eyes. But those eyes had been blind to everything around him. Maybe that was simply the way of the world; the narcissism of children was a well-known fact. Whatever the reason, he had not noticed, and, Junior, well, he had no particular dedication to religion.

Another noise from above broke his reverie and he listened-in again until he was satisfied that Eldon had settled back down into his chair to watch — whatever it was he was watching on the television upstairs. He put out his cigarette and lit yet another as he turned back to the letter.

> *Papa is still working at the school and Mama continues to take care of him and the little ones (who aren't so little any more.) I visit with her every Wednesday and take her down to get the cheese that the government gives away at the center near where they live. They get by on what Papa makes, but he doesn't give her much money for the house. I think he drinks most of what he makes away. So, Mama is always trying to figure out ways to make her money stretch from paycheck to paycheck.*

"Typical," Junior thought. The old bastard was still a drunk. Some things never change. If Papa Jesús was more concerned about taking care of his family and less concerned with his tequila and his *verga,* then so much of everything that had happened would not have occurred. As these thoughts entered his mind, Junior felt a warmth rising in his belly. A warmth that he knew would ignite if he let it fester. He put thoughts of his father away and returned to the letter.

> *Lucia is married and living in Austin with her husband. She has two little boys. Sometimes, she doesn't seem very happy, but I don't know why. She has a husband and those two boys — what more could she want? What more could any woman want?*

Junior reflected on the last time that he had seen his oldest sister, Lucia. It was the day of the shooting, but Junior barely recalled it. Angelina had run up to the Big House to get Lucia so that she might help in the aftermath of Hector's destruction. The last thing that Junior recalled at that time was sitting in the back of the old pickup truck, his hand wrapped in wet cloths while his other sister, Luciana, lie in the bed of that truck as they were carted off to the hospital. As they drove away, he watched his eldest sister (who in some ways had been more of a mother to him than Mama Fabia had been) standing at the front of their home as she faded away.

For a moment, he felt a throbbing in his non-existent fingers; that throbbing that was often referred to as "phantom pain" but it did not feel like a ghost to him. Along with the pain, the temperature in his belly began to rise.

Gus has started school here. It won't be like when we were all out picking in the fields. He won't be missing school to work. He will be able to spend every day there. Hopefully, he will grow and learn so that he can get a good job. It's not like the labor jobs are around as much as they used to be. Things keep changing and we have to change with them.

Junior reflected on how lucky he had been to find Eldon and Emma. That these two good people had taken him in, so many years ago was a miracle. That Eldon had bestowed upon him the gift of his mechanical knowledge was a blessing. Junior had learned from his surrogate father more than he could have dreamed possible in those days when he was harvesting cotton for another. His newly gained knowledge would ensure that he might find employment in something other than the fields. Sure, that employment would still involve using his hands (and he chortled at the thought of his hands) but it was meaningful and gainful employment nonetheless. The thought of his hands increased the phantom pain and the heat in his belly began to itch.

As to Luciana, well, what is there to say? She pretty much lays in her bed all day watching television. Sometimes, she makes up stories that she tells to Lucia's children. Sometimes, she tries to write those stories down, but with her hands the way that they are, she has a hard time doing so. I pray to God for her each and every day. I pray that He makes her better or helps her to find peace with her lot. If He chooses to keep her from walking, well, that must be His will. Who are we to question God's plan?

Mama took Luciana to see a bruja a couple of months ago. She swears that the witch's magic will break the spell that keeps her from walking, but I know in my heart that God will not reward her for dabbling in that evil. Pastor John says that those who seek comfort from a demon will not find their path to salvation. That can only come from a deep and abiding love of Jesus Christ — the kind that I have deep in my heart. Maybe if Luciana could find that too, she would get better. But she will never get better if she keeps going to witches to solve her problems.

He was aghast to learn that Mama Fabia took Luciana to a *bruja*. What was some witch doctor going to do for her that all the men with the fancy degrees could not? That his mother would even consider such a thing spoke to the depths of the woman's superstitions. That his family refused to come to terms with the situation — a situation caused by Hector, but that had originated with Papa Jesús's own failings as a husband — incensed him.

Junior extinguished his cigarette in the ever-growing pile of butts in the ashtray. He heard another thump from upstairs and paused to listen as he lit yet another. There was no more noise from above, and so he returned to the missive.

You were asking about Papa in your last letter. He is the same. He hasn't changed much. He goes to work cleaning the school every day and at night he goes out with his friends. Mama doesn't like that he keeps drinking so much, but what can she do about it? So, she puts up with it and continues to be . . . well, Mama. Some things never change, I guess. If they were to find a clearer path to the Lord, then maybe it would, but I feel that if they keep doing what they are doing nothing will never change.

The only path to righteousness is through the love of Jesus Christ. Papa doesn't beat on Gus like he used to do with you. Maybe it's because he is not having to work to bring in money the way that you had to. But he does get angry sometimes and when he does, I know that he still hits Mama. But I don't really know about that, or even what is going on with them. I guess she is used to it and just accepts it. I am not sure if I could.

I wish that you would come home and visit. I wish that you would let me tell everyone where you are and that you are okay. Even if I don't tell anyone else, please, please, please let me tell Luciana. She worries about you and would love to know that you are ok. Can I just tell her that? I don't have to tell her where you are or what you are doing — only that you are ok. Think about it and let me know.

Forgiveness is what is important, right? Jesus teaches that forgiveness is the way and that man cannot find heaven except through Him, right? We all need to forgive. That includes you, Junior. I know what our padrino did was a terrible thing, but you must learn to forgive him the way that Christ forgave the men who put Him to the cross.

Forgiveness! It was so easy for Angelina to speak of forgiveness. She could still walk. She still had all of her fingers. The thought of forgiving Hector disgusted him. How could he ever forgive that man? It was because of Hector that Luciana was in the condition that she was in and it was because of Hector that Junior had no fingers. He felt the heat in his belly inflame.

In disgust, Junior threw the letter down and stood up, knocking the chair that he sat on to the floor behind him.

"Damn it," he muttered to himself as he turned to pick up the chair. At that moment, from above, he heard a loud thunk on the floor.

"Eldon?" he called out and waited for the old man to answer. When none was forthcoming, he called out again, but still received no response.

"What, now?" Junior said to himself irritably as he tossed the chair up against the desk, then turned and started up the stairs to see what had happened.

"Hey," Junior called out as he entered the living room of the apartment upstairs, "What's going . . ."

He stopped himself when he saw Eldon slumped over and ran to the chair. He noted that Eldon's breathing was thready as the older man clutched his left arm with his right hand.

"Hold on," Junior said, "Hold on. Come on, I got you."

He helped the old man up out of the chair through the front door and down the stairs to the front of the garage and to his Fairlane that was parked in its usual spot. He maneuvered Eldon into the front passenger seat then ran around to the driver's side as he pulled his keys from his pocket.

Falling into the driver's side seat, Junior quickly pushed the keys into the ignition and turned the engine. It roared to life without complaint, as it always had.

"Just hold on," Junior said again. "I will get you to the hospital in five minutes."

Then he peeled out of his parking spot and onto the road that took him to the interstate and to the hospital that was very close by.

Back in the garage, the partially lit cigarette that Junior had tossed into the ashtray rolled away from atop the mountain of butts it rested upon and onto the desk, just on top of Angelina's letter that Junior had haphazardly tossed aside. The paper on which the letter was written began to smolder.

"I am sorry," the doctor said. "We did everything that we could."

Junior looked at the man in the long white coat.

"What does that mean?" he asked. Although he knew the answer, he could not bring himself to accept it until the doctor said it outright.

"This was his third heart attack; the second one in the last two years."

"I know," Junior responded. "So, go wake him up."

"I am sorry,"

"No. No. No," Junior shook his head, cutting the doctor off and pointing back down the hallway. "Go wake him up."

"Unfortunately . . ."

"Don't. Just stop. You go back there right now and you wake him up," Junior insisted plaintively.

"We tried everything . . ."

"No, you didn't. You couldn't have. Go back there right now."

"I am sorry."

"Don't say that."

"He is gone."

"Stop."

"There is nothing more that we can do."

The heat that had been threatening to erupt in his belly raged from the fissure that had been made in his broken soul. For a moment, he envisioned himself punching the doctor in the face and beating it to a bloody pulp, but when the doctor placed his hand on Junior's arm, the spell was broken and the heat subsided. Junior slumped onto one of the plastic chairs that lined the hallway and put his face into his hands.

"Someone will come down to speak with you about what to do next," the doctor said.

He looked up at the man, his eyes were red as he fought back the tears that threatened to flood and nodded his head.

In the parking lot, sitting in his car with his hands on the steering wheel, Junior sat looking through the windshield. He had not yet turned the engine. He simply stared at . . . nothing.

"How could this have happened?" he asked himself. "What could I have done?"

He looked down to the passenger seat at his right and at the bag that held the items that Eldon had with him when they first entered the hospital; his "personal effects" the hospital staff called them. Junior reached down and put his hand atop the bag almost caressing it. Then, he snatched that bag by its corner and flung it off the seat to the footwell. Reaching up, he banged his hands three times on the steering wheel punctuating each hit with the words. "Damn it! Damn it! Damn it!" He stopped, took in a deep breath, and stared silently through the windshield.

Across the parking lot, he watched a little, old woman making her way to the front door of the hospital accompanied by what he could only assume was the old woman's son. As he watched he thought . . . well, he did not know what he thought. His mind was blank yet, still it roiled in thought. When he caught himself, he wondered, "How can a man spend so much time thinking about nothing?" As he watched them walk, their progress hardly registered in his mind.

Taking a deep swallow, he inserted the key into the ignition and turned the engine. As it had always done, the car immediately came to life. But Junior did not. With the car running, still, he sat in its driver's seat staring through its windshield thinking about . . . nothing.

He must have sat there, paralyzed for some time, because the next thing that registered in his mind was the old woman with her son now leaving the hospital. In the time that it had taken that woman to enter and leave, he had done nothing but sit and stare; all the while the car's engine running and emitting fumes.

Before he drove off, he reached down to the footwell of the passenger seat and picked up the bag that contained Eldon's "personal effects". Carefully, he placed the bag on the seat and lovingly caressed its top.

He sniffed-in to prevent the mucus from running out of his nose and wiped his eyes with his left hand, then put the car in gear and drove out of the parking lot.

It was less than five miles from the hospital to the garage, so the trip did not take long, but the minutes passed like hours, and he hardly noticed the sights around him as he turned down the street toward his home.

"My home," he thought. "Is it really my home anymore?" Now that both Emma and Eldon were gone what was to become of the little garage? What was to become of his "home"? While at the hospital, Junior had been so lost in the present that he had not thought to consider the future. What was to become of the garage? What was to become of his home? What was to become of him?

Deep in the pit of his stomach, Junior's fear began to build. It had been so long since he had been on his own; so long since he had been alone; he was not at all certain that he knew how, anymore. The fear fluttered in his belly and began to stir, then the heat began to build.

As he turned onto the street that led to the garage and the apartment above, he noted a number of firetrucks. When he came to the corner that ultimately led him to his home, if, in fact, it still was his home, his way was blocked. Down the street, he saw the firemen working diligently to douse the flames that had overtaken the garage; his garage; his home — if it was his home — and he shook his head to clear his thoughts.

Junior meant to stop the car. He intended to get out, and run to the garage, but when he pulled over, he could not move. He sat with his hands frozen to the steering wheel watching through the windshield.

"Damn it! Damn it! Damn it!" he cursed again through gritted teeth punctuating each with a bang on the dashboard. Even from this distance, he felt the heat of the flames, but that heat did not burn in the same way as the fire in his belly.

The whispers in his head became howling shouts of anger and pain. He felt the fury begin to overtake him.

"This is all so unfair!" he wanted to shout. He wanted to raise his fist to the air and curse God for letting this happen. "It has always been this way! What did I ever do to deserve this?"

The whispers in his head were screaming now, "This is Hector's fault! This is all fucking Hector's fault! Everything is Hector's fault! First Luciana, then the hand, then Emma, then Eldon and now *toda esta mierda!* All of this shit is because of Hector!"

The howls in his head screamed to him that the letter from Angelina would never have come had it not been for Hector; the letter that sparked the embers in the garage and now sparked a conflagration in his belly. It was ALL because of Hector!

Junior banged his fists on the steering wheel again, this time to the drumbeat of the whispers.

"Hector!" they said and he banged on the dashboard.

"Hector!" (Bang).

"Hector!" (Bang).

"Hector!" (Bang).

"Hector!" (Bang).

Then the howling in his head ceased. All was silence and no sound tickled his eardrums.

Then, he heard the whisper. "Odessa," it said.

Nodding silently in assent, then to himself aloud, Junior repeated, "Odessa."

He turned the key and ignited the engine, not knowing, or even seeing what he was doing. He simply obeyed the whispers in his head.

Junior turned his car around and drove back the way he came. He drove down the road for the entrance to the Interstate, up its ramp and toward the East.

CHAPTER 15

"I get that oil pays more, but with auto work at least you are guaranteed to continue to work no matter what's going on," Tommy repeated. "I mean, people will always need their cars no matter how high the price of oil or gas, right?"

"True, but I gotta admit I like the money in oil a lot more," Junior laughed as Daniel and Johnny raised their glasses in a toast to the money. "And if the oil work goes bust, I can always work on cars until the boom comes back."

"Boom!" Johnny cried out as the other men at the table roared in laughter. Other patrons in the bar turned to see what was so funny. This only made the men at the table laugh more. Clearly, they felt the effects of the alcohol.

"Like I said, I was pretty good at it," Junior continued. "But it was time to move on. After the old man passed, he left the garage to me. But I was young and didn't want to stick around in El Paso. You gotta remember, this was back in the early seventies and I was still young, only twenty-three or so. I wanted to get out and spread my wings. I sold the garage and left. I wanted to see other places. I wanted to do . . . something.”

“I get it,” Tommy said. “We all gotta find ourselves.”

“Fuck that hippy-dippy shit,” Johnny interrupted. “Only thing a man’s gotta find is a way to make a living; to put a roof over his head, food in his belly, and clothes on his back.”

“What about the love of a good woman?” Daniel asked.

Johnny replied, “Well, I don’t know about ‘love’, but a man sure enough needs some good-lovin’,” then he laughed at his own witticism.

“This from a man who’s been married what? Three times?” Junior asked Johnny with a sly grin.

“Marriage ain’t for everyone,” Johnny shot back. “Never could get used to having someone underfoot all the time.”

“But we all need someone,” Daniel said.

“For what?” Johnny sneered. “Women are a dime a dozen and, like that country singer said, ‘you can find ’em anywhere.’”

“And that’s why your wife left you: Because you couldn’t afford the dime,” Junior interjected to the laughter of the other men.

“Nah,” Johnny replied. “Truth is she couldn’t handle all of this.” Johnny waved his hand, palm up from the top of his head down to his chin indicating his face to which each of the men laughed drunkenly again.

“So,” Tommy interrupted. Getting the conversation back on track, he turned to Junior and asked, “did you?”

“Did I what?”

"Find yourself . . . or whatever it was that you were looking for."

"I found a good woman. As to the rest, let's just say that I'm still looking."

Junior recalled that Hector had gone to work the oil fields. So, when he arrived in Odessa, he applied for that type of work anywhere and everywhere he could. It was not until the day that he entered the offices of one company or another that the receptionist told him he was wasting his time. She pointed to a stack of applications that sat on the corner of her desk.

"If you want work," she said, "you gotta go up the road apiece to Midland. Don't bother filling out no applications. Just find the nearest field and ask the boss there if he's got some work."

Junior took her advice. As he drove, in the distance he saw the familiar sawhorse pumps that were busy pulling black gold from the ground. Whenever he saw a group of men standing by, or near, one of these pumps, he stopped to inquire about work. It was three days later when luck finally struck and, like the oil that erupted from the ground, work spurt forth. He found a job about twenty miles outside of Midland. The two-man crew had not shown up and it was well into the afternoon shift. The lead at the site looked him up and down until his eyes came to rest on Junior's hand.

"What makes you think you can handle it?" the driller asked.

"Ain't no machine stumped me yet," Junior replied. "Ain't nuthin' done stopped me; and ain't nuthin' ever will."

The driller nodded, then asked, "You read and write in English?"

"Better than most, not as good as some, " Junior responded.

The driller let out a small laugh,"I guess you will have to do, then."

The work itself was dangerous, and it took Junior some time to get the hang of things. The missing fingers of his left hand did not make the work any easier, but years of adapting had shown Junior the way to make-do with the tools that remained at his disposal. The driller took notice and brought him along to the new sites where they installed the equipment necessary to pull that Texas tea from the ground.

For the next few years, Junior worked these pumps in and around Midland/Odessa and all over West Texas. He proved himself to be a hard-worker and valuable asset for any team to which he was assigned. Even if at times he was prone to what might be considered reckless behavior, that daring helped the crews finish on time or ahead of schedule. He became much sought after on different crews. Whispers of some of his more daring exploits spread through the company. Junior learned that he had gained quite a reputation and that many had taken note. But he did not care about his reputation or his notoriety. Each day, he put in his time and worked harder and harder, returning at the end of the evening to whatever little place he happened to be camping-in that night to take long showers in vain attempts to remove the stench of the day's work. And each morning he rose to do it all again.

But wherever he went, whatever he did, he always had his eyes open in search of Hector. For the past many years, despite all of his searching, he had seen neither hide nor hair of the monster.

Three or four years after taking his first job in Midland, and three hours into this particular shift, Junior was replacing a worn-out bit. He threw the steel slips to keep the pipe from falling down the hole, then used the tongs to unscrew the pipe.

The drilling floor was exposed to the sun with only a small canvas canopy set up at the far end near the lead man's old pickup truck. Under that canopy, the crew stored water and other things that might get in the way of the job. The heat was unbearable under the Texas sun, and every so often Junior had to remind himself to drink more water.

This crew consisted of five men. Well, four men and one woman — an unusual situation in the early to mid-1970s.

Derrick was the lead. He was a big man, but all muscle and no fat. In his early to mid-forties, he had thinning blond hair and hailed from somewhere back East, but had been working for the company, as he described it, "Since, God was a boy."

The other two men were locals about Junior's age (i.e., their mid-twenties), Patrick and John.

Patrick had red hair and claimed that his family had immigrated from Ireland in the last century. Junior did not know much about Ireland, nor did he much care, but the man was ghostly white under that red hair and Junior marveled that he never cooked under the Texas sun.

John claimed to be Kickapoo but, again, Junior did not much care. The man had longish black hair and skin even a darker brown than Junior's own.

Finally, there was Ginny, the sole woman on the crew. She had short, dark hair and very light skin. She claimed to be a mix of Native American, Mexican and White and had startling green eyes. Because she had worked for so long in a field dominated by men, she had broad shoulders and masculine musculature. She had been working the industry since she was 19, or so she said, about three years, now, and was one of the first women to break into this man's world.

Because she was a woman, the men often teased or played pranks on her. Like the time that she had used a port-a-potty at one of the sites. As soon as Patrick saw her enter the little blue hut, he quietly snuck up to the door and padlocked it. Several minutes later, when Ginny, now finished with her business, tried to leave that commode she discovered that she was sealed in.

While the men outside roared in laughter, using language that would make a sailor blush, she yelled, cursed, and shouted at them. But nobody came to her aid. So, she banged and kicked on the door until finally, the structure teetered. When it tipped over (with Ginny still inside) the din of the men's merriment was loud enough to drown out even the sound of Ginny's continued blue language.

By the time that she managed to free herself, she was covered in the spilled human waste that had escaped its compartment and flowed freely within the overturned hut.

Ginny stepped out, seeing red. One look at Patrick's face confirmed that he was, in fact, the culprit, and she ran to him, then punched him squarely in the jaw.

Patrick was more than mildly surprised by the violence and had not even tried to duck when her fist connected with his jaw. He fell back and onto the ground while a reeking Ginny stood over him fuming. The other men quickly rushed to restrain her from meting out any further punishment.

Patrick sat up, rubbed his jaw, then said, "Damn, Ginny! That's one helluva right hook you got there."

"Better be glad your compatriots here are holding me back," she spat.

"I'm sorry," Patrick said. "I didn't think it would tip over."

"Yeah," Ginny said, "well it did."

"I'm sorry," Patrick repeated.

"You best just keep away from me the rest of the day."

"That shouldn't be a problem," John said as he wrinkled his nose at the stench coming from her and smiled.

Ginny replied with a look that shot daggers from her eyes and made his smile quickly fade.

Patrick rose from the dirt and wiped his jeans with his hands. "I didn't think that would happen."

With a finger pointed in his direction, Ginny replied, "You best watch yourself."

John and Junior sniggered a little at this before Derrick intervened. "Enough," the crew leader said. He looked pointedly at both Ginny and Patrick. "We done here?" he asked.

"Yes, sir," Patrick replied.

"Good, then get back to work." He turned and walked away.

"I really am sorry," Patrick said again as he rubbed his jaw. "But damn, girl! You really are one tough bitch!"

"Better than being just a little bitch like you," she retorted. Patrick's eyes widened in surprise while John and Junior guffawed at her response.

The crew returned to work while, grinning, Junior looked over at

Ginny. At that moment, he made the decision: "Someday," he thought, "I'm gonna marry that woman."

Several months later, Derrick was driving as the crew returned from a site about sixty miles outside of Midland.

Ginny sat in the front passenger seat while Patrick and John passed bottles of Lonestar beer back and forth. Junior, tired, slept in the back seat.

"So, tomorrow morning we gotta go up to Pump 15," Derrick was saying between swigs of his beer. "Company says it ain't pumping right."

"Any idea what the problem is?" Patrick asked from behind.

"Not yet. We gotta assess it when we get there." Derrick let out a large belch, then tossed his bottle of beer through the open window watching and waiting for it to break.

"You're disgusting," Ginny said.

"I got my charms, though," Derrick replied.

"With charms like that, ain't no wonder that your wife left your sorry ass," she retorted and the other men in the truck laughed. She knew that she probably should not have said such a thing, it had only been three months since Derrick's wife left without warning, but Ginny was not one to hold her tongue.

Derrick replied, with a smile on his face, "Now that I'm free and single, maybe you wanna have a go?"

"I wouldn't fuck you with one of their dicks," she responded with a toss of her head toward the back of the truck. Again, the men in the truck burst out laughing.

"Ain't asking for a fuck," Derrick replied. "Just put your lips together and . . . blow."

"If I was dying for air and the only source was in your balls, I still wouldn't suck your dick," she responded.

Again, the men in the truck burst into laughter — even Derrick, although he had been the butt of the joke. Shaking his head, he raised another bottle of beer in Ginny's direction, looked over at her and said, "You are too much."

Ginny grinned back, then turned and looked out the windshield.

"Watch out for the pig!" she cried out.

Derrick saw the javelina a split-second later. That Ginny had mistaken the animal for a pig did not surprise him. Javelinas are found as far south as Argentina and as far north as Texas, New Mexico and Arizona. But unlike their porcine cousins, they are even-toed hoofed mammals and are often mistaken for pigs.

What did surprise Derrick was that these thoughts ran through his head in the seconds that it took for him to yank the steering wheel to the right in an attempt to miss hitting the beast. But standing as it had been in the middle of the road at the curve, Derrick's reaction was too late and, quite likely too much. The truck veered right as the javelina ran left. The back end of the vehicle slid forward and the truck rose up onto the wheels of its left side.

For the briefest of moments, it seemed that the vehicle might right itself, but before it did, it slid into the berm, and then hit a pile of dirt that had been placed as a break.

They flipped over and rolled down the side of the raised roadway. The truck flipped not once, not twice, but three times as it rolled down that embankment.

Junior awoke from the jostling and felt his head hit the ceiling of the vehicle as it rolled downward. Inside the front, Ginny screamed as Derrick cried out, "Oh, shit! Oh, shit! Oh, shit!"

The rear passenger door opened and John was thrown from the vehicle as it continued to roll down that hill.

When the vehicle finally came to a rest, Ginny slumped over the dashboard. Derrick groaned from the driver's seat, and Patrick looked down at a leg which was bent into the most improbable of positions, looking, for all intents and purposes, like one of those crazy contortionists one might see in the circus.

Junior was jostled and shaken, but otherwise fine, having suffered only minor cuts and bruises. He looked out the window and saw John limping toward the vehicle.

Everyone crawled out of the vehicle, everyone except for Ginny. She struggled to catch her breath and seemed unable to move.

At the sight of her, Junior's mind flashed back to that early morning so many years ago. For a split-second, he did not see Ginny at all. He saw his sister lying on the ground unable to move as she struggled to catch her breath. The non-existent fingers of his left hand began to throb, then that vision quickly faded and he made to help Ginny exit the truck, but she was unable to get out of the seat.

Junior stopped and looked at his face in the now-cracked mirror. Minor cuts and bruises, but nothing major. He hurt all over, but did not seem to be too seriously injured. Neither did John. The pair pulled Patrick from the back seat of the vehicle and John helped to splint the other man's leg as Junior sat with Ginny.

"It will be alright," he said. "We'll flag someone down."

It was two hours later before they were able to do so; two hours before someone finally stopped in an old pick-up truck and carried them off to the nearest hospital. They were among the longest two hours of Junior's life.

From a payphone, Junior called their employer, PermaCo Oil, who sent a representative to pick them up and care for their needs.

By tacit agreement, Junior claimed that he had been driving the truck — there was no sense in getting Derrick into trouble. If their employer discovered that Derrick had been drinking while he drove the company truck, he certainly would have been fired. Junior, on the other hand, had nothing to drink on that drive. No matter how many tests they ran, those tests would come back clean. So, he agreed with Derrick's suggestion.

For a week, Ginny remained in the hospital as the doctors patched-up her broken ribs and other injuries. At the end of that week, it seemed clear that she would not return to work anytime soon. Desperate to ensure that he did not lose this woman from his life, on the last day of her hospital stay, he got down on one knee and asked her to be his wife.

CHAPTER 16

"What happened to Jesús and his family?" the priest asked.

"On the morning of the accident," Alejandro interrupted himself as he re-thought what it was that he was saying.

"Can I really call it an accident? Let's be honest. It was not an accident. I shot her. I may have been out of my mind. I may have been possessed by a demon that used my body to commit its evil, but it was not an accident."

He continued, "On that morning, Luciana was taken to the hospital in town, but it was a small hospital and they could not help her. I know that she, and her family, ended up in Austin; and I know that thirty years since the monster stole my body, Luciana remains unable to walk. As for the others, I really don't know. I only know about Junior.

"When *La Furia* relinquished my body, she entered Junior and took over his; maybe even his soul as well. That morning, Junior lost three fingers on his left hand. The three middle ones; the result of getting caught between the hot iron of the pot of beans and the flames of the stove. It has become not only the mark of the boy I once knew, but the mark of *La Furia*, as well. It is that mark that I see when the monster is near. When I see a man with the disfigured hand, I know that it is the monster coming for me in the guise of Jesús's son."

Alejandro — the man who had once been Hector — thought about the last time he had known for certain where Junior was — back when he was in Midland, Texas.

Alejandro entered his office and sat in the chair. Within moments, his assistant entered carrying a cup of coffee that she set down on the corner of his desk.

"Thank you," he said. "Were you able to pull that file I asked for?"

"I requested it from Personnel. It should be here soon. I will follow up."

"Thank you," he said, again. As she exited his office, he called out to her, "Please close the door."

"Certainly," she replied and closed the door behind her.

Alejandro brought the hot coffee to his lips and took a sip. Looking at his surroundings, he thought. "I would hate to have to give all of this up."

It had not been an easy time for Alejandro and Carmen in those days immediately following David's death. Although clearly the result of an accident (or, as was Alejandro's own belief, a self-inflicted wound), there had been numerous legal loops to jump through in order to ensure that Alejandro maintained control of the mineral rights that were the very basis of the lease that would make him rich.

David had died intestate, but he had no heirs and his only next of kin was his widow, Carmen. Everything that he owned, passed to her. Alejandro had naturally insisted that the partnership agreement contain a clause within it to ensure that, in the event of the untimely passing of either partner, the land and all rights thereto, passed on to the surviving one. Thus, he now owned 100% of the land and its rights.

"Isn't it ironic," he thought, "had I waited only a few more days to execute the lease, I would have inherited it all anyway."

Then again, he wondered, if he had not swindled David out of his share of the lease, would David have died? It was easy to assume that David's death was the direct result of the divorce proceedings, but more likely than not, it was the combination of losing his wife, his income, and all assets associated with the lease that caused the destructive behavior that ultimately led to that death.

There were many nights, especially those immediately following the accident, when Alejandro was racked with guilt over what had occurred. On those nights, he was unable to sleep — not out of the guilt that he felt, but out of fear; fear that the nightmares that plagued him might return; fear that *La Furia* herself would come to claim her due. But that did not happen. Whatever magic emanated from Carmen's presence next to him in bed, kept the demon at bay.

The probate proceedings had slowed down the lease, but it is amazing what smart lawyers backed by the bottomless bank account of a top oil company can accomplish when the promise of future treasure dangled before them.

Now that Alejandro was the undisputed owner of the land in its entirety, and with the threatened litigation over each partner's respective percentage of those rights was dead ("As dead as David," he thought) there was nothing to do but wait.

To ensure that Alejandro would not shop his lease to their competitors, PermaCo Oil gave him a hefty signing bonus and offered him a position in their executive offices to, as they put it, "See him through" until such time as the wells produced their promise. That position came with a fat salary — more money than he had ever made in the entirety of his life. Because he had no experience in a corporate office but had secured his reputation in the field, the company moved him into a position where he could help oversee production operations. Over the course of the next several years, he proved himself to be a valuable asset and excelled in his position.

But, there is an old saying that life interferes when a man makes his plans. And so, it was with Alejandro. The confluence of life's currents did, indeed, intervene when he heard rumors about a daring roughneck.

This employee had shown up only a few years before and had made quite a reputation for himself. A reputation for being a hard worker who could, and would, get anything done that needed doing. He was respected by the men with whom he worked because of his can-do attitude and his willingness to take on any job — no matter how big or how small, how demanding, how difficult, or how dangerous. His derring-do quickly became the stuff of legend among the other men.

But he also had the reputation as a man who held a deep-seated anger always simmering just below the surface. A man who might react at a moment's notice with violence against any perceived provocation, real or imagined.

Despite having this man under his employ, Alejandro had not met him. It's not as if he spent his days out in the field. His days were spent in the comfort of a well air conditioned office. He was curious to learn more about the other man. He was curious to find out for himself whether the rumors were true. But, more importantly, he was curious to learn about the man's rumored, and all too familiar, disability.

Alejandro took another sip of his coffee when he heard a light knock at his door followed by its opening. His assistant walked in with file in hand and set it down on the desk in front of him.

"Here is the file you asked for," she said.

"Thank you," he responded and waited until she had left and closed the door before he looked down at the file on his desk.

"Could it be?" he wondered and opened the folder.

The man's personnel file had scant information within its pages — little more than his personal data and a very sketchy outline of his past experience.

As Alejandro sat in his chair poring over the details, he found an interesting report about a car accident that occurred in the Basin. Alejandro had a vague recollection of that accident and the ensuing discussions within the halls of the executive offices, but he had to read the entire report in order to refresh his memory. A quick perusal confirmed that this was the incident he recalled.

It occurred when a team was repairing a well that had been down for a broken spinner. It had been a long and difficult job and when they were returning to town, the accident happened. Three men and one woman had been involved. Alejandro mused that perhaps that is why the report had stuck in his memory. It was indeed rare for a woman to be working the field and the woman, he looked down at the paper to confirm her name, the woman,

"Ginny," had been seriously hurt. There had been a nice payout at the time to recompense her and she had not returned to work thereafter. The company had considered the matter closed and never followed up.

Alejandro put the file aside for a moment and sat back in his chair as he tried to jog his memory for details about that incident. He recalled that there had been concern that those involved had lied about the accident, and that it was caused, not by the employee who accepted responsibility, but by another — someone else who had been driving.

There were conflicting reports about who the actual driver had been. While one of the employees insisted that the driver had been another named (and he looked at the file to refresh his memory) Derrick, the man whose personnel file lay before him now, had insisted that he had been the driver. This employee accepted full responsibility while Derrick insisted that he was not the driver on that night. Since they could not persuade him to admit otherwise, they had no choice but to accept his word and that became the official story despite any rumors to the contrary. Those involved in the investigation determined to accept the official report and, once the woman accepted the payout, the matter was put to bed.

He mused on the information that he had read. Was that the reason this employee engendered such respect and loyalty? Not because of his feats of daring, rather, because of his willingness to protect his teammate? To accept blame and potential consequence for an action that one had not committed presented a loyalty to one's team that might, indeed, breed its return.

To himself, Alejandro wondered whether the opposite might also be true. If accepting consequences for something one had not done in order to protect another bred respect and loyalty, what did the failure to accept consequences for one own's actions engender? Contempt?

He thought to himself, "That which we put out returns to us three-fold. Love begets love. Hate provokes hate. Violence returns violence. Loyalty engenders loyalty. We get what we give."

Then he wondered, "What will return to me?"

Alejandro looked back to the file at the emergency contact information, and quickly realized that this employee later married the woman. Naturally, this piqued Alejandro's curiosity.

He continued to read, looking for information about the man's rumored disability, but all that he found was a cryptic note from the employee's supervisor that read: "Despite his fingers, Junior is able to outperform most of his peers."

Alejandro sat back in his chair and put his hand to his chin lost in thought.

"What does that mean?" he wondered, "That part about 'his fingers'? Could it be? The name is so common. It might be, but then again, it might not. How can I find out for certain without tipping him off, if, in fact, it is him?"

He steepled his fingers in front of him and pressed his upraised index fingers to his chin as he sat and thought.

"If it is him, does he know that I am here? Does he realize who I am? If it is him, how did he find me? If it is him, what is being returned to me?"

Back to the file, he looked down at the man's hire date. Shaking his head, he considered, "It can't be. He has been here far too long. If it is him, he doesn't realize who I am. He would have confronted me long ago if he knew."

He wondered, "But what if he is only biding his time? What if he does know and is just waiting to . . ."

"To what?" he interrupted his own thoughts. "What would he do? Call the police? So, what? My papers are too good. Nobody has ever questioned them. I could deny it all and then what could he do? But if they look closely enough, if they start to investigate, what then? Would the police discover the truth?"

Of course, nobody had done so before, but this was different. If there was an accusation of murder, and, if the man was who Alejandro thought he might be, then, well, then the police would be very thorough; far more thorough than a cursory check into the life of the man known as Alejandro.

An ice-cold fear gnawed at his chest. "I could lose everything," he thought. "Everything; the job, the money, even Carmen."

That thought was more than he could bear, and he heard, softly at first, the chittering of the monkey demand, "Feed me!"

The monkey's demands became louder as he sat in thought until he shook his head to evict those urgings. He brought the coffee cup to his lips only to find that the liquid it held was now cold. He reached down and buzzed the intercom on his desk and asked his assistant for more.

"How can I be certain?" he wondered.

Alejandro's assistant entered and handed him another cup of coffee. "Will there be anything else?" she asked.

"No, thank you," he replied, but as she turned to leave he stopped her.

"Wait," he said and she turned around.

"I want you to find," he looked back down at the file running his finger down the page until he saw the name of the employee's supervisor, "find John McCrary and let him know that I would like to speak with him."

"Certainly," she responded and left the room.

"Well," he thought, "maybe this McCrary can shed some light on this."

He closed the folder on his desk.

CHAPTER 17

"Well, you definitely got a good woman in Ginny, that's for sure," Johnny said.

As Junior lifted his beer in a toast to the other man, the door of the bar opened and three men, talking loudly, walked in. It was obvious by their carriage and demeanor that this was not the first establishment that they had visited this evening. With narrowed eyes, Junior watched as one of the men made his way to the bar while the other two found seats near the pool table and commandeered it for a game.

Johnny caught Junior's gaze, looked over his shoulder then back to Junior and muttered, "Oh, fuck; those assholes again."

"Yep," Junior said as he took a sip from his beer.

"Who are they?" Tommy asked.

"That's B-Crew," Johnny replied. "A bunch of damn idiots."

"Why do you say that?" Tommy asked.

"They take stupid short cuts that almost always lead to problems we gotta fix."

"They aren't all bad," Daniel interrupted. "Alberto's a pretty decent guy."

"That won't last," Junior said. "Decent guys don't make it very long in that bunch. Either he'll lose his job, get hurt, or become just like the others."

"Birds of a feather," Johnny said.

Junior's group watched as B-crew began their game of pool. As they did, he overheard Derrick say to another that he was not properly motivated.

He grunted at the phrase and his thoughts turned to the last time he saw his father.

"I am making *mole de pollo*," Ginny said to her husband as he entered the door to their Midland home.

"Ok," Junior replied, "but not that chocolate one, the peanut butter one, right?"

"Of course," his wife replied.

"Good," Junior said. "I hate that chocolate shit."

"You have another letter from your sister."

"Ok. I will read it after I change."

Junior walked over to his wife as she stood at the front of the stove, wrapped his arms around her waist and kissed her on the side of her neck.

"Stop," she said laughing and pushed him away. "Dinner will be ready in about half-an-hour. Go clean up. You stink."

Junior grinned widely.

"What are you grinning at?" his wife asked.

"I was just remembering the time that Patrick locked you in the port-a-potty and you tipped it over trying to get out. I don't smell half as bad as you did that day."

Ginny laughed and gave him a light smack on his shoulder. "I may have stunk back then, but you reek today."

"It's the smell of love," Junior replied with a smile.

"It's the smell of oil," Ginny responded.

"It's the smell of money," Junior shot back.

"If you own the well," they said in unison and then laughed together.

"I'll be back in a bit," he said, and trudged down the hall to shower and change.

Despite his care-free attitude with his wife, in the shower, as he cleaned himself, Junior seethed. It had been a long and hard day. One of the pumps had broken down and they had been unable to fix it. The head office was angry and was sending another crew to see what they could do. Junior's crew was re-assigned, but that might take a week or so; a week without work.

Junior sat at the kitchen table and began reading his mail. He casually looked through various bills which only seemed to be getting higher with each new month. He made a mental note of the amounts due, then considered the amount that he knew to be in his checking account. With each new bill that he opened, the seething anger within him grew.

He set aside the last bill and turned to the letter from Angelina.

> *July, 1979*
>
> *Dear Junior,*
>
> *I know that it's been awhile since I wrote, but things have been hard lately. I don't know what to do or who to talk to. I am writing to you because I have to confess to someone and you are the only one that I know of who won't tell anyone else.*

Confess? What could she possibly be confessing? Ever since she got involved in that church years ago, she had been so careful about not doing anything that she thought might be a sin.

> *I have sinned in the eyes of the Lord. A very grievous sin and because of what I have done, Lazlo has moved out of the house. God willing, we will patch things up and he will come home. I just don't know if he will ever forgive me for what I have done. I don't know how to say this, so I will just come out and say it: I am pregnant again and the child is not my husband's.*

Junior sat back in surprise. Angelina cheated on her husband! Of all the things that he might expect from her that was the last of them. Given her holy roller attitude these many years (sometimes bordering on holier-than-thou) that she would succumb to such a base instinct was, indeed, surprising.

Putting her convictions aside, had she learned nothing from Papa Jesús's infidelity? Did she not realize that it was their father's inability to deny himself those particular pleasures that ultimately led to the tragedy that was now Luciana's life? Did she not see the correlation between Papa Jesús's action and Junior's own loss of fingers? Knowing all of this, how could she give in to that particular temptation?

I don't know how it happened. Lazlo was working so much and I was lonely, but that is no excuse. We had been fighting more and more. I was angry with him for working so much and leaving me alone at home. I know that I should not have been angry. Anger is a road that leads to the Devil. Work is important and he was only caring for our family. But I needed him to be here, to be around more. Out of anger and loneliness, I spent more and more time at the church while Lazlo was working and I grew closer and closer to Pastor John.

We didn't mean for it to happen! It just did. The Devil whispered in our ears and we gave in to the temptation that we felt. I thought that we had been careful, but now I am pregnant. I could not even pretend that it's Lazlo's because he and I have not been together as man and wife in almost as long. I feel terrible about what I have done and I am greatly ashamed. I have come clean with Lazlo, so he knows everything.

As you can imagine, it has caused quite a problem between him and his brother. Lazlo was so angry that I was afraid. I worried that they were going to get into an actual fistfight! I worried that Lazlo might let his anger overtake him and hurt his brother.

Obviously, they are not talking, now, and Lazlo has been very upset with me. I don't blame him for that. I was in the wrong. I admit that. He is staying at this parents' home. but we have been talking every night. I have begged him to forgive me and told him that I would do whatever he wants if he will forgive me.

At this point, I don't know what more to do besides get down on my knees and pray to God to make everything all right. I do that every night now. I hope that this confession to you doesn't make you hate me too.

As he read the letter, Junior's mind wandered to the morning that he caught Papa Jesús with his godmother, Mariana. How his own view of his father had certainly changed that day. He considered the heartache and shame that the old man's actions had caused. He thought about how that infidelity led to Hector's rampage. He understood Lazlo's anger just as he understood Hector's, but understanding the 'why' does not lessen the impact of a man's deeds.

As he considered these things, Junior felt the heat in his belly begin to itch.

I still have not told anyone that we have been writing, so nobody knows that we are in touch. I suppose that you will want to know what's going on with everyone else.

I think you know that Lucia is returning to Texas with her new husband. Her third! Can you believe it?

You remember I told you that her first husband, Rand, hurt her and the boys. None of us knew about it except maybe for Mama. I think that Lucia told her about it, but you know Mama — she told Lucia to put up with it because the Church would not condone divorce.

Isn't it funny that Mama just sat back and let Papa beat on her and you without saying anything and that Lucia swore that she would never marry a man that did that. But of course, she did.

And, isn't it funny that Papa always cheated on Mama and even though as a little girl I swore I would never be anything like him, now I am — having cheated on my own husband. I guess the apple doesn't fall far from the tree, after all.

I don't know. I am so confused by things right now. Bad husbands hit and cheat on their wives and we women are supposed to sit back and take it.

Then here I go: I have a good man in Lazlo and I do what I did. Nothing makes much sense anymore and I know that I'm just rambling on here.

Junior stopped for a moment feeling somewhat disgusted with what he was reading. The old memories and feelings that had been lurking within for so long; the ones he thought dead and buried since his marriage to Ginny, began to rise within him.

He felt queasy as the heat in his belly rose and began to burn.

Gus is not doing so good in school. He is flunking his classes and he has been running around with a bad crowd and skipping school. Mama got very angry with him and finally got it out of him that he is gay. When Papa found out, he beat Gus to within an inch of his life, and told him that he would not have that in his house. He threw him out. I don't know where he is or what he is doing. Mama says he ran off to Florida. I don't know. Of course, being gay is wrong and God would not approve, but Papa should not beat him over it. They should take him to a church so that he can find his way back to Jesus and away from his sin. But you know Mama and Papa, they don't think that way.

Junior had only dim memories of his youngest brother. The boy was hardly old enough to walk and talk when Junior ran away. At this point, he must be what — nineteen or twenty?

Whatever may have happened in the intervening years, Junior certainly could not speak to. He had no experience with homosexuals, except for what he may have seen or heard on the television or in the comments, mostly derogatory, from the men with whom he worked. The only thing he knew for certain was that he did not want to be around one of them. But this was his brother — even if he did not know the boy anymore, blood is thicker than water.

Besides, regardless of how he felt, that was no reason for Papa Jesús to beat his younger brother. Having been on the receiving end of his father's lashings before, Junior knew more than a little something about it.

Although he did not condone Gus's choice in lifestyle, he bemoaned that anyone, let alone his brother, should be beaten by a parent for it; beaten by a parent for anything, for that matter.

As these thoughts crossed his mind, and as he recalled the beating that he endured as a child, the heat in his belly began to consume him.

Luciana is the same as she has always been. She stays in her bed and watches telenovelas all day. We can't even get her to get into her wheelchair to take her out. Sometimes, we have to fight with her just to give her a bath. When she is not watching those telenovelas, she writes poetry. Some of it is pretty good, but when I read it, it makes me so very sad. The words that she writes make me realize how lonely and scared she really is. I try and tell her that there is nothing that can be done. She will not walk again and that must be God's will, so she simply has to accept her fate and make the best of it.

Then she starts talking about how she is really a dancer and I don't understand. How can I? I just keep telling her that she needs to find her way to Jesus, but I think that only makes her angry at me for telling her. What else can I do though? It's the truth. Maybe if you wrote to her she might feel better? Please think about it. I know that she wants to hear from you. She misses you. You two were always so close. Just knowing how well you are doing might make her feel better.

As he thought of his sister, Luciana, Junior's anger boiled. His beautiful sister simply languished in bed, unable to find love, peace, or any other thing that each and every woman should be entitled. She would never know the joy of marriage or children. She would never have a life of her own that did not involve lying in that bed watching those stupid telenovelas.

Along with the boiling anger, came the return of the whispers — whispers that he had not heard since marrying Ginny. But the whispers were demanding attention this evening.

"This is Jesús's fault!" they said. "It all goes back to the father and his sins."

> *Papa is Papa. Nothing has changed there. He is still mean to Mama. He goes to work every day and goes out every night with his friends. We all know what he is doing, hanging out with the painted women on South Congress, but nobody can or will say anything to him about it. Of course, given what I have done, who am I to say anything?*

Junior threw the letter aside and saw the corner of the paper flutter. In his mind, the corner erupted into flame.

The whispers in his head became more insistent.

"This is Jesús's fault," they said.

"This is Hector's fault," they said.

"This is the fault of evil men who do evil deeds," they said.

Junior felt the heat within consume him in much the same way as the fire that had consumed the garage where once he had worked and lived.

"Yes," Junior said aloud to himself in answer to the whispers. "Evil men who do evil deeds."

And the whispers replied, "They must be stopped."

"Yes," Junior repeated.

He did not know where Hector was or how he could find his godfather, but he knew where Jesús was. Thanks to Angelina's letters, he knew this very well. It would not be difficult to find the old man.

"He must be stopped," the whispers said again.

"Yes," Junior replied, then slowly nodded his head. He thought that, perhaps, it was time to pay his father a visit.

Carefully, he folded the letter and returned it to its envelope. For a moment, he sat at the kitchen table hearing his wife's chatter, but not listening to what she was saying.

"I have to go to Austin," Junior interrupted his wife.

She stopped what she was doing at the stove and turned around.

"What's wrong?" she asked.

"My Papa is sick," he said. "I have to go to visit."

"Do you want me to come?"

"No," he said.

"I have never met your family. Why don't you want me to?"

"How perceptive she is," he thought. The idea of subjecting his wife to the misery that was his past was too much.

To Ginny, he replied, "It's not that I don't want you to meet and get to know them . . ."

To himself, he thought, "Well, now, that's a lie. I don't want her anywhere near them."

To his wife, he continued, "I, just . . . well, you know that I haven't spoken to any of them, except for my sister, Angelina, in all of these years. They are . . . how do I say it in English? *Moro viejo nunca será buen cristiano.*"

"Ah, stuck in their ways and unable to change? The literal translation makes no sense in English," she replied, then, "You have to have grown up with Spanish to understand, I think."

"I don't want to subject you to them."

"But I do want to meet them. And, if he is sick, maybe I can help."

"No," he repeated. "There is no need. I am just going to see for myself how sick he really is. If I need you, I will call you and let you know."

Junior knew there was nothing that she could do to help him with what he knew needed to be done.

"How long are you going to be gone?" she asked.

"I don't know. Probably just a couple of days, but it could be a couple of weeks. Depends."

"Leave," Junior said to the plump woman in the bed. The stained sheets and polyester coverlet barely covered her.

"He still owes me," she insisted as she stood and began to dress.

"That's not my problem," Junior replied. "You can take it up with him another time."

The old hooker began to protest, but when she looked into Junior's steely eyes, she thought better of it. From behind the door to the bathroom, Junior heard the water from the shower stop.

The old hooker looked at him once again as if to protest further, but with a flick of his head, she scurried out the door of the seedy room of the South Congress Avenue hotel and silently closed it behind her.

Junior sat in the scuffed-up chair in front of the desk — so small that it hardly could be called a desk at all. He covered the lamp with a cloth subduing the light that emanated from it, then he turned the chair to face the bathroom door. He sat, and carefully settled his right hand, the one that held the gun, into his lap.

As he walked out of the bathroom, Jesús said, "*Yo no tengo el dinero que . . .*" but then stopped short when he saw the man sitting in the chair. A quick glance around confirmed that the hooker was no longer in the room. Assuming that the man in the chair was the hooker's *chulo*, Jesús said, "I got the money."

"I don't care about that," Junior replied. "Sit down over there on the bed."

Jesús reached down to pick up his pants, but Junior stopped him with the words, "Leave them. Let's talk a bit."

Warily, Jesús looked back at the man. Junior saw the look on his father's face change to a look of acquiescence when the old man spotted the gun in Junior's lap. Jesús sat on the corner of the bed, towel wrapped around his waist. "What do you want?" he asked.

Silently, Junior looked Jesús up and down and noted the yellowed and missing teeth. He wondered why any woman would have interest in being with this man. Obviously, the interest here was the money that Jesús had brought with him.

Jesús shifted in his seat discomfited by Junior's stare and asked, "What do you want?"

"Does it bother you?" Junior asked.

Jesús looked at him quizzically. "Does what bother me?"

"I'm just curious. When you leave here after putting it to one of these whores, do you go home and fuck your wife?"

Jesús was taken aback by the question, "What do you mean?"

"Does it bother you to do that?"

"To do what?"

"We are going to be here a long time if you don't stop acting stupid," Junior said waving the gun toward Jesús.

"My question is: Does it bother you to go back to your wife after fucking one of these whores?"

"What do you know about my wife?"

"Does it bother you to do that?"

"I don't understand," Jesús replied.

"Do you see the whore's face when you are putting it to Fabia or do you see hers?"

"When I'm putting . . . How do you know my wife's name?"

"Does it bother you?"

"Why do you care?"

"What about your children?"

"My children?" Jesús asked, obviously confused.

"Do you ever think about them?"

"What do my children . . ."

"Do you think about them?"

"I don't understand!"

"Do you ever wonder whether your daughter — the one lying in the bed unable to walk — do you ever wonder if she knows or suspects what you are up to?"

Junior saw Jesús's face fall. He was clearly unnerved by Junior's information.

"How do you know about her?"

"Do you wonder if she knows who you really are?"

Jesús stared back at this man that he did not recognize. Junior saw the expression on the old man's face as he tried to puzzle it out. That his father did not recognize him only gave fuel to the burning fire in Junior's belly.

He heard the whispers again, "What are you waiting for?" They demanded to know. But Junior was not yet ready to release his prey.

"Do you think about her?"

"*Por favor. Yo no intiendo que . . .*"

"Don't give me that shit," Junior interrupted with a wave of the gun. "You understand. I bet you '*intiendo*' a lot more than you let on. Do you always play the 'me-no-speaky-English' card when the questions get difficult?"

"What is it that you want from me?" Jesús whined plaintively.

"What about the boy? The one you threw out? Do you think about what kind of lessons you were teaching him?"

"What boy? How do you know about my children? How do you know about my wife?"

"I am just wondering; Does it bother you?"

"*Mira,* I don't know what you want, but, look, I got the money to pay. I was gonna pay." Junior heard the desperation in the old man's voice and through that desperation, the whispers in his head grew louder.

"Yes," they said, "you've got him now."

"Yes," Junior replied to the whispers, and then to Jesús he responded, "You are going to pay."

"I don't know what you want!" Jesús insisted. "Just tell me what you want."

The whispers in Junior's head grew louder, "Can you taste his fear?" they asked. Junior nodded in reply.

To Jesús, he said, "You don't recognize me, do you?"

"Why should I? Who are you?"

"Let me tell you a story."

"I don't want to hear a story. Please, just let me go. Take whatever you want and go. I won't come back."

Ignoring him, Junior continued, "A very long time ago, there was a little boy who wanted only to please his father."

On his face, Junior could read his father's confusion. The old man still had not put two-and-two together.

"What docs . . . I don't . . ." Jesús replied.

"That little boy was marked because of his father's actions, though. Marked in a way that would forever haunt him."

"What are you talking about? Just . . . Look, the money is in my pants. Take it all. Take what you want. Just let me go."

"Do you mean those pants?" Junior asked using his left hand to point with his pinky at the clothing that lie crumpled on the floor.

He followed Jesús's gaze as it moved from his elbow, down the length of his forearm, and, finally, to his hand. He saw the realization dawn in Jesús's face when he came to that mangled hand and he almost read the thoughts that danced behind his father's eyes as he looked back at the man sitting in the chair.

When there was no doubt in Junior's mind that Jesús now recognized him, he smiled a thin smile at the old man and the whispers silenced.

CHAPTER 18

In the confessional, the priest asked, "Did you see him again?"

"Yes," the old man replied. "I was working for the company — the very one that I had sold my lease to — and I heard rumors that there was a man with the mark working for us. At first, I did not believe that it could possibly be Junior. How could it be, after all of these years? For the past decade, I had been hiding in plain sight, and nobody had ever questioned who I was. But I was frightened. If it was him, then everything that I worked for, everything that I had sacrificed, was all in peril. So, when I heard the rumors, I started to investigate. I had to be sure."

"What did you do?"

"First, I pulled his personnel file to see if there was anything in there that might confirm my fears. But there wasn't really — not much, anyway. There was a short reference to something about his fingers, but . . . nothing that I could point to." A small grunt escaped his lips as he pondered on the idea of pointing with no fingers.

"Junior's name, his real name, his full name, Jesús Gonzalez, was too common to be sure. There are thousands of Jesús Gonzalezes across the state. How could I be certain that it was him?"

"So, how did you confirm?"

"I met with his supervisor. I wanted to ask about him. I wanted to be certain. I asked him to describe the man that worked for him."

"What did he say?"

"He said that Junior was a hard worker and a valued part of his team. But that is not what I really wanted to know. I didn't care about what kind of an employee he was. I only wanted to know if this man was the boy that I once knew."

"How could his supervisor confirm that?"

"Obviously, he could not. But he could confirm the mark."

"The mark?"

"The mark of *La Furia* — the missing fingers. So, I asked the man point-blank if his employee had any disability, and he confirmed that the man who worked for him was missing the middle three fingers of his left hand.

"And I knew. There was no doubt in my mind, anymore. I knew. The marked confirmed it. This employee; this man was, indeed, the boy that I had known. He was the very same Junior who I had hurt so many years ago.

"What are the odds of that, *Padre*? What is the chance that almost two decades after the incident this boy, this man, would find me?"

"Perhaps, God wanted you to meet him again," the priest replied.

"Oh, no, *Padre*," Hector said shaking his head. "This was not God's doing; not at all. I knew then and I still know today — that was not the work of God."

"God works in mysterious ways . . ."

"No," he insisted. "This was not God's doing. This was the work of *La Furia*."

The priest furrowed his brow and asked, "What do you mean?"

"The morning of the incident; that morning when my very own hand betrayed me and shot those children, I saw her. I watched as she left my body and entered the boy. She took control of that child at that very moment as surely as she had control of mine before.

"Maybe she had been looking for me all of these years, hiding inside *mi ahijado,* or maybe she had known where I was and had only been biding her time, while hiding in my godson, but it was her. This was the handiwork of *La Furia,* and I was frightened. I was so afraid that she would slip out of Junior and back into me.

"Perhaps, I should have been more concerned about the child, Junior. But like the coward that I was, I was more afraid that she would exact revenge on me. I had escaped her clutches once before. I was scared that this time, I would not be able to resist her dominion."

The priest thought a moment, then asked, "Have you considered that she is nothing more than the manifestation of your own guilt?"

"It was not guilt that first brought her to me, *Padre*, and it was not guilt that brought her back. No. It was vengeance. It was anger. It was wrath. She is the Goddess of Vengeance and Wrath. Those were the sins that opened the door to her possession and those are the sins that continue to invite her in."

"What happened then?"

"I did what I have always done. I ran."

"I don't understand," Carmen said to Alejandro. "Why do we have to leave so quickly?"

She stood in their living room watching as her husband paced to and fro as he tried to make his case for moving.

He stopped and looked at his wife, "The opportunity is there now and I want to take it while it is. If we wait, it may not come again."

How could he tell her the true reason he wanted to escape Midland?

"But what about Michael? I don't want to take him out of school."

"Our son is young, he'll adapt," he said with a dismissive wave of his hand.

"But . . ."

"Carmen, I understand your reluctance, but this is a great opportunity for us."

"We don't need more money. The royalties from the wells are more than enough to . . ."

"It's not about the money!" Alejandro snapped.

It was not his intent to be so terse, but with the confirmation that the employee was indeed the child that he had maimed so long ago, he worried that he might be found and caught.

To Carmen, he said, "I am sorry."

Alejandro sat on the sofa next to her and took her hand, then continued, "I'm sorry. I don't mean to be hard. But, I am not thinking about money. It's about leaving a legacy; leaving something for Michael. It's about the future. Those oil wells won't pump forever. Sooner or later they will go dry. Whether they go dry in fifty years or in ten, or tomorrow, we don't know. But I want to leave something for my son to call his own." Alejandro marveled at how easily the lies passed his lips.

"But do you really want to sink everything we own into this pipe . . ." and she struggled to come up with a descriptive ". . . dream? What do you know about running a foundry?"

"I know as much about that as I knew about oil wells when I first came here. I know as much about that as I knew about love when we first met. I will learn. I can hire those who know more to take care of what I don't know, and I will learn from them too."

Carmen looked at him curiously. He could tell that she was considering his behavior. He had to admit that behavior was, indeed, odd and he could not fault her for noting it. She was a perceptive woman, after all. But he needed to persuade her to go with him. He did not want to go alone, but leave he must, if he were to escape the clutches of the demon yet again.

"Look," he said, "I really think that this is a great opportunity for us. I am going to Houston to check it out this week. Come with me. I think that you will like being near a city with so much more than what is here in Midland. We can turn it into a little get-away for just the two of us. Your sister can watch Michael. I will check out the plant and look more into the deal. If we decide to move forward, I will go ahead and secure a house and take care of all the details. You and Michael can follow after the school year is finished. And, if you don't like it, then we won't do it."

Carmen did not want to seem unreasonable, so she acquiesced to Alejandro's request.

"I did what I have always done. I ran." Alejandro said to his confessor.

"I went home and considered all of my options. I knew that I could not stay in Midland, but I had to figure out a way to convince Carmen to come with me.

"I learned that the foundry was for sale and I took that opportunity to persuade her. We bought that foundry, packed up our home, and came here; to this sleepy suburb not far from the center of Houston.

"With that, my transformation was complete. Hector ceased to be and Alejandro began the third act of his life. Alejandro became the man you know: the businessman who is respected by his colleagues and employees; the dutiful husband; the devoted father; the church-going man; the philanthropist known for his generosity. Alejandro is the man that Hector could only hope to be. If only it were not all a lie.

"And, so, there you have it, *Padre*. That may not be the most grave of my sins, but it is definitely the most pernicious; the lie. I guess that if you think about it, each and every one of my sins boils down to theft. First, was the theft of truth."

"God will forgive once you confess and repent."

"Will He? I wonder. Are there not some sins that are so . . . horrible, so terrible, that even God Himself must turn away?"

"There is no transgression that He will not forgive. If you are truly remorseful and ask forgiveness with utmost sincerity."

"I wish that I could be as certain as you, *Padre*."

"There is nothing that He will not forgive."

"How can you be so sure?"

"He gave his Son so that you may be forgiven."

"And where has that gotten us?" the old man asked, momentarily lost in philosophical musing about the plight and nature of man.

He continued, "I don't know, *Padre*. I don't know. Sometimes sins, well, they eat away at a man. They eat away at his very soul.

"It doesn't happen overnight, you know. But each sin leads to another that leads to another and it continues on and on without end. Each sin, no matter how insignificant it may seem, destroys a small piece of the soul. Each new sin grows greater than the last and as the sin grows, the part of the soul that it destroys and erodes grows larger, too.

"What happens when the sins have grown so large that they finally devour the soul? What happens when there is nothing left? Can He forgive a man who has no soul?"

"Every man has a soul, my son. It cannot be taken away."

"Even those who have repeatedly lied to Him?"

"Without exception."

"I don't know. Yet, still, I am here seeking absolution and forgiveness. I come here not as Alejandro, the old man that you know, but as Hector, the one you do not. It is Hector who must confess and who must do so now, this very night."

"Why the urgency?" the priest asked his charge.

The old man drew a deep breath. "For so many years, the young man, Hector, has hidden inside the body of this old man before you. For so long now, he has tried to escape the sins of his past. But even in his hiding, he always knew that someday, someone would come along and see through the window of the old man's eyes deep within and find the frightened younger one hiding. That happened tonight, *Padre*."

"What do you mean?"

"I don't know how, but she found me."

"Who found you?"

"*La Furia*. Who knows how long she has been hunting me? Who knows for how long she has driven the boy, Junior, using his body to search for her prey — the one that got away? Does it really matter? Because, tonight, it happened."

"What happened?"

"I saw her tonight. I saw her in the eyes of the little boy, Junior, only now fully grown; that little boy who is no longer Jesús's child, but the vessel for the demon that preys; the body that has been consumed by that demon. And when she looked through his eyes, I knew that she found me, Hector, hiding way down and deep within Alejandro.

"I knew that there is no more escape, no more running. I knew that I must confess."

"Is there more that you wish to confess?"

"Isn't that enough?"

"You have confessed your sins to God, Alejandro, but you know that is not enough. You must also atone."

"What prayers are there that a man can recite to atone for a lifetime of sins?"

"I will give to you your penance, but you know that is not enough."

"Atone?"

"You must turn yourself in to make up for what you have done."

"'Render unto Caesar', *Padre*?"

"God must have his due. But so must man."

"Oh, I know, *Padre*, I know. But even that may not be enough to escape the monster."

"No monster can outrun a man with a true and abiding faith in God."

"Oh, but *Padre*, you don't understand," the man who once was Hector, then Alejandro, and Hector once again, said. "Can I outrun myself?"

"What do you mean?"

"I am the monster."

CHAPTER 19

In the bar, Johnny said to Tommy, "You see the short one in the red shirt?"

"Yeah."

"He's their lead; name's Derrick. They take their cues from him, but they are cut from the same cloth."

"What kinda shortcuts?"

"Well, there was this one time that Derrick sent one of the men down to the belt for some maintenance, but he wouldn't shut it down. He was afraid of losing production. The worker slipped and his sleeve got caught in the belt. He was able to wrench it free, but if he hadn't, he might've been dragged down the belt and had his arm ripped off.

"Another time, he didn't properly secure the spinner. We took over later that day and, when we did, the chain broke. It might have taken out someone's eye as it whipped around if that someone had been standing too close."

Tommy whistled, "That was pretty stupid. Still, accidents do happen."

"Yeah. They happen alright, but they seem to happen more often with that lot than with any of the other crews. I heard Derrick's been given a good talking-to on more than one occasion — not that management really gives a damn. They are only concerned about getting the job done and the product out. If someone loses an eye, I guess they consider that acceptable losses."

"Kinda cynical there, ain'tcha?" Tommy asked through a grin.

Johnny harrumphed, "You'd be a cynic too, you lived my life," and he raised his beer in a toast while the other men laughed.

"Junior knew Derrick from before," Johnny said, then turned to Junior, "Didn't you?"

"Yep," Junior said taking another swig of his beer, then, "He was a drunk even back then."

Daniel asked, "He worked drunk?"

"Sometimes. Mostly it was after shift, but not like we are here now having a couple of beers in a bar. We was working the Basin and drove from well to well. Mostly, he got drunk riding home."

"That wasn't very smart," Daniel remarked.

"Nope. But in the seventies, nobody gave a damn if you were drinking and driving. That shit didn't start 'til the eighties with Mothers Against Drunk Drivers."

"Fuck them," Johnny said raising his beer, "Here's to Drunks Against Mad Mothers," and the men let out hearty laughs.

Junior continued, "Management would have been pissed off if

they knew he was drunk the night of the accident, but they never knew."

"What accident?" Tommy asked.

"Didn't I tell you that story?" Junior asked. "Me and Ginny we're working a crew with him."

"Ginny worked on a crew?"

"Yeah. That's how we met. Anyway, she and I were working on a crew with Derrick. He was driving us home. We were on a long, lonely stretch of highway and Derrick was downing one beer after another until he crashed the truck."

"Wow. Was anyone hurt?"

"We got banged up pretty good. Ginny was in the hospital for a while. She never did get back to work and, in fact, we got married shortly after that."

"Did he get canned?"

"Nope. I was still young and dumb and, well, kinda looked up to him, I guess. So, when the suits asked, we told 'em I was driving. I had been sleeping in the truck and hadn't been drinking. If we had told them the truth, likely Derrick would have been fired. So, I took the blame. Of course, nothing happened to me. They chalked it up to just an accident and let it go. After that, though, Derrick kinda avoided me. It wasn't until the day he fucked up again on the job that the shit hit the fan."

"What happened?"

"Same shit. Derrick was drunk and didn't do what he was supposed to do, and I almost lost my head."

"What did you do?"

"I kicked his ass — that's what I did. Unfortunately, that got me fired."

The early 1980's brought a recession to the United States despite the optimistic outlook of her new president. That recession began in 1980 and continued through 1982 and its effect had now hit Junior's employer in Midland. But that was not the only reason that he lost his job.

The company that had been drilling since the 1930s, sold to another, PermaCo Oil. It was not long before senior executives flew in and started making changes — and these changes were not for the better. They cut staff, but still insisted on raising production. They eliminated quality control and safety inspectors. They refused to hire relief workers. The company demanded more and more work from less and less people. They moved from three eight-hour shifts to two twelve-hour ones.

To cut costs, PermaCo placed restrictions on safety equipment and that equipment became harder to find. What once was normal operational procedure, such as shutting down machines for maintenance, lengthened the downtime taking away from production activity.

While management continued to discuss the importance of safety, those discussions were mere lip service — and the supervisors who might be tasked to enforce such safety measures felt increasing pressure to forego them in the name of production and the Almighty Dollar.

While profits increased and management was happy, the workers were more than a little agitated by the new order. In order to meet the demands that were being heaped on them, they took shortcuts to meet their production quotas. Derrick was one of the worst offenders. Increasingly, accidents occurred.

Junior's crew was working on the mud tank of one of the wells out in the Basin. Mud tanks are divided into different tanks depending on the shape of its bottom. Its surface is made of slip-resistant steel plate and the surface of the tank is equipped with a water pipeline for cleaning the equipment on the tank (using soaked zinc processing.) Some of the compartments have agitators that contain long impellers inserted into the tank for stirring the fluids. Mud guns spray high-pressure mud into the fluids to prevent precipitating. A suction line links the mud tanks with mud pumps.

On this particular day, Junior's crew was tasked with cleaning the pumps and replacing a worn impeller. This crew generally consisted of five men, but since recent cutbacks, they were down to only Derrick and Junior along with one of the pumpkinheads (new employees, so-called because of the orange hats that they wore). The fourth man had not shown, and the crew was down from its usual complement since the company refused to send a replacement worker.

In Junior's estimation, most of these new men were worthless, especially this one. It was not that they were unable to perform the job at-hand, but these replacements had little to no experience. Moreover, they were not working the job because they enjoyed the work, but rather they did so because they needed a job — any job in the current recession conditions.

This frustrated Junior to no end. How were they supposed to complete the jobs assigned to them if they did not have the men with the proper skills, training, and temperament to do so?

They were nearing the end of their shift, but the impeller was wobbling.

"Ready?" Junior asked Derrick as the pumpkinhead packed up to move out.

"Almost," Derrick replied. "I just want to tighten this up a bit."

Junior walked over to the control box to stop the equipment when Derrick said, "Let it be. It'll take twenty minutes to restart and I wanna get out of here. This won't take but a minute."

"But it ain't safe to . . ." Junior started before Derrick interrupted.

"It'll be fine. I do it all of the time."

"I don't think that . . ."

"Leave it be," Derrick ordered again. "I wanna get this done."

"Do you want it done quick, or do you want it done right?" Junior asked.

"Both," Derrick responded. "It won't be a problem. Just get your ass over here and give me a hand."

Against his better judgment, Junior acquiesced. Derrick was the boss on this team, after all.

With cigarette dangling from his mouth, Derrick used his wrench to apply the necessary torque to tighten the impeller.

As Junior watched on, he felt uneasy at the sight of Derrick's hand so near the moving parts of the equipment. He felt a tingling in his missing fingers — that phantom pain, once again. Junior pulled his left hand back and opened and closed it into a fist (as much of a fist that a man can make with only a pinky and thumb on his hand) to alleviate the sensation in his nonexistent digits.

The butt slipped from Derrick's mouth, but its end remained adhered to his lower lip fastened by some unseen glue. When he reached up to pull it free, his glove snagged on the moving piston and Derrick pulled his hand out of the glove an instant before that glove hit the pipe, saving the fingers of his right hand.

But when that glove hit the impeller, one of its blades broke. That blade flew out and up and square into the front of the hardhat that Junior wore. An inch or two lower, the man with no fingers may very well have become the man with no face — the poster child for plant safety.

Derrick's jaw dropped as he gulped in fresh air and Junior fell back. The blade that might have taken Junior's face, indeed, his life, was easily seen jutting from the front of the man's hardhat.

For the moment, Junior was stunned, then he sat and pulled that hat off of his head as quickly as he could muster tossing it to the side.

"Thank God for the hat," was all Derrick thought as he ran to Junior.

But, the other man's shock did not last long. The tingling that had begun in his nonexistent fingers turned to a bright, white heat that travelled up his arm and down his torso until it enveloped him.

Junior pushed Derrick back and away from him, rose, then charged with fists flying. Knocking Derrick to the ground, Junior straddled the other man pounding into his face over and over again. The heat within him burned brighter with each and every impact of fist to face.

Junior had not been at work the day that the pink slips went out. He was on suspension after the fight with Derrick and on the day that he was meant to report back, he was, instead, summoned to the company's offices in town.

Not knowing what it meant that he had been called in, Junior felt anxious as he entered the reception area. Little trails of sweat dripped from his brow down the side of his face, but he was not at all certain whether the sweat was from the Texas heat or from his nerves. He announced himself to the woman behind the desk who asked him to take a seat as she picked up the phone to let another know that he had arrived.

When the assistant came to reception, he followed her down the hallway toward the conference room where he had been directed. On the walk, he chatted with his escort.

"Tough times," he said to the petite blond.

"Don't you know it," she responded. "You're not the first to be summoned by the old man."

"Think anything is gonna change?" he asked.

"I wouldn't bet on it," she said. Then stopped in the hall and turned back to him.

"Look, Junior," she continued, "So many have come in here asking about their future here, and, well, to be honest, it's just not going to happen. Until this recession settles down, I think we are all in a fine kettle of fish. You didn't help yourself when you got into a fight."

But Junior did not hear her as she spoke these words. His eyes had been drawn to a picture hanging on the wall behind her. That framed photograph showed two men in front of a pump. The men were standing and holding their tools. One wore his hardhat, but the other did not. This was the one that caught his attention.

Despite the twenty or so years that had passed, there was no mistaking him, even though the man in the picture was bald, missing a tooth, and sporting a scar across his eyebrow.

He looked nothing like the man that Junior once knew but there was no doubt in Junior's mind. Hector might be able to change everything else about himself, but he could not change his eyes. In those eyes, Junior saw the monster that once had invaded his home.

Still, he had to ask, "Who is that?"

"Who?" the assistant asked, then turned to look at the picture.

"Those men there; who are they?"

"That's Mr. Melendez and one of his friends from way back when. They struck oil out in the Basin and sold the field to PermaCo years ago."

"Melendez?" Junior asked suddenly questioning his thoughts.

"Yes. That was taken before Mr. Melendez married and joined the company."

"When was it taken?"

"Oh, gosh, that must have been ten or fifteen years ago."

Nodding, Junior thought, "That sounds about right."

To the woman, he said, "I thought I knew him. Are you sure his name is not Hector?" Junior said.

"Oh, no; that's Alejandro. I knew him pretty well. I was his assistant for almost five years," the woman said.

Junior looked over at her and asked, "But you're not anymore?"

"He moved away a few years ago. He and his wife went on down near Houston."

"Houston, you say?"

"Yes; well, actually one of its suburbs or somewhere thereabouts."

"Is he still there?" Junior asked.

"I believe so, but he left here several years ago. I don't think he is the man that you think he is. His name was Alex — er, Alejandro — not Hector."

"Of course, you are right. It can't be the same man I knew."

The assistant looked at him quizzically.

"I just remembered something," Junior said quickly. "I gotta go."

"But I thought that . . ."

"That's ok. Just have them mail me the paperwork. I really have to go. I forgot about an important meeting."

"Ok . . ." she said hesitantly. "Let me . . ."

"It's ok," Junior said. "I can find my way out," then he turned and almost ran down the hallway to the exit.

CHAPTER 20

The men at the table laughed at Johnny's bawdy joke about the hooker and the pirate as Junior pulled his bottle of beer toward his mouth to draw another swig. Halfway to his mouth, he stopped and stared at the front door of the bar.

Through that door an old man walked in. Although it had been almost thirty years since the morning that Junior had lost his fingers, there was little doubt in Junior's mind who that old man was. Sometimes, there was no disguise to hide the true nature of a monster.

Even as Junior continued to smile, the laughter in his eyes faded away. The grin that he wore morphed into an altogether different one; one that was much more malevolent in its nature. His eyes hardened as he watched that old man belly up to the bar and he felt a burning deep within.

Junior brought the bottle to his lips and drained it in one swallow. He continued to laugh and joke with his friends, but all the while, his eyes never lost sight of the old man who sat at the bar.

It had been a hard day for Alejandro.

Earlier, he had an argument with his son, Michael, about the future of his business. Michael, now in college, was not content with the idea of taking over the foundry. The younger Melendez wanted to sell the family business to PermaCo Oil, a company that had, if truth be told, made a very fine offer. But Alejandro did not want to sell to his former colleagues. He had built this company from the ground up with his very own two hands and intended it to be his legacy for his son. But his progeny had no interest in that legacy. Instead, he was more interested in the financial windfall of selling. This dismayed Alejandro.

Why couldn't Michael see how much it meant to him that the boy take over the reins of the business when he retired? All of those years of back-breaking work to turn his little pipeline foundry into something that he could be proud of, something that he could pass on to his son, would be for naught if the boy had no inclination to continue the business.

Then again, if his son was not interested, he could not force him to do so, could he? Did any father have the right to force his child along a path that child did not want to traverse? Maybe, when all was said and done, Michael was right. Why not sell and make a nice profit for his golden years? He and Carmen were not getting any younger. Why not enjoy the time left in a relaxing retirement?

But this was not the only thing that Alejandro worried on this evening. There had been the accident in the yard. One of the men carelessly drove his forklift into a stack of piping. That piping came down and injured another. What this meant for his workers' compensation premiums was anyone's guess, but there was no doubt that they would go up. It likely also would precipitate a visit from OSHA officials wanting to investigate the accident bringing with them all of the red tape and business disruption that entailed. All that meant was more headache.

But the truth is, well, the truth is that Alejandro could endure these headaches had it not been for the tales he heard coming from the yard. The stories about the worker with the missing three fingers; the worker who just might bear the mark of *La Furia*. It had been so very long since last he heard of someone with the mark that he had almost forgotten about it — almost.

He had not seen hide nor hair of Junior in these many years, and the last he knew, Junior was in Midland. He wondered, "Could the monster have found me again, after all of these years? Was this man they spoke of . . . Junior?"

How many men were working in this industry with only a pinky finger and a thumb on their left hand? It had to be Junior. Who else could it be? It could not be mere coincidence.

Like in Midland before, a growing fear ballooned within him. If Junior had found him, *La Furia* was certain to follow on his heels.

By the end of the day, Alejandro felt a thirst that he had not felt in such a very long time. Before he had even realized what he was doing, he slipped out of his office and wandered down the street to the nearest bar.

He thought that the monkey was gone; the one that had clung to his back for so many years. But tonight, the monkey reappeared, and it was chittering incessantly in his ear demanding to be fed.

Against his better judgment, Alejandro walked into the watering hole that he knew many of his men frequented. He told himself that he had no intention of succumbing to the monkey's desires, but when he left the office that evening, he was drawn to the bar.

He insisted that he was going only to listen to the conversations of his employees so as to get a feel for the morale of his workforce. But deep inside, he knew that was a lie. Just another one of those lies that he told himself so often to justify his own behavior. In truth, his desire to go to that bar was to assuage the need of the monkey and to silence its pleas.

When Alejandro walked into the bar, he looked around. It was not full, but neither was it empty. There was a nice crowd for an early evening; large enough for him to get lost in, but not so large that nobody would see him. Still, there were enough people that the men might not all realize who he was or even that he was there.

From the entryway, Alejandro saw the few empty stools at the bar and, quickly, he made his way to one of them as he continued to listen to the pleas of the monkey.

"Feed me," the monkey whispered into his ear.

"Feed me! Feed me! Feed me!" the monkey repeated with incessant need.

Alejandro's hand began to shake with the tell-tale signs of his submission to the monkey's need.

At the bar, he took a stool and ordered a tequila shot with a beer chaser. The bartender brought him the drinks and Alejandro placed a twenty-dollar bill on the bar.

He sat and stared at the drink, but the better angels of his soul stayed his hand. He watched that beverage, neither picking it up, nor drinking, but watching the cool soothing liquid sit in the still of the glass. The pool of liquid at the rim of that glass chased his mind into reverie, but that reverie was broken by the loud cries of the monkey now demanding more than ever to be fed.

One of the workers, bellied up to the bar and sat on the stool to his right. The man had the stench of sweat and oil that often pervaded the very pores of these workers, and Alejandro winced at the odor. With a small shrug, he reminded himself that this was the smell of money and that he should not be so quick to take offense.

"*Hola, jefe,*" the man said to him and clapped his left hand to Alejandro's left shoulder in a too familiar gesture.

Alejandro felt the monkey scurry across his shoulder to the other side and whisper into that ear, "Feed me. Feed me. Feed me."

"*Hola,*" Alejandro said to the man wishing he would remove his hand from his shoulder, but not wanting to push the man's hand away. He did not want to even look at the man's arm for fear that he might offend one of his workers during this perilous time.

To the man, he said, "I don't know you. Are you one of the new men?"

The man reached down into the bowl of peanuts that sat before him and gathered a handful that he quickly tossed into his mouth and chewed.

"Not so new," Junior replied after he swallowed then ran his tongue against the front of his teeth. "Been with the foundry for a little over a year."

Alejandro smelled the rank odor (that stale scent of too much alcohol) on his employee's breath, but kept himself from reacting.

"So far so good?" he asked the man.

"It seems to be working out. More so than ever today, I think," and

Junior smiled at Alejandro as he reached down for another handful of peanuts.

"How so?" Alejandro asked.

Through a mouth full of nuts, Junior replied, "Let's just say that it's been a good day, and I think that it will only get better."

"From your lips to God's ears," Alejandro responded.

"Any truth to the rumors about PermaCo?" Junior asked the old man.

To himself, Alejandro wondered how any of his men could have heard the rumor.

To Junior he asked, "What rumors might those be?"

Junior grinned back and said, "Come on, *jefe*, you know the rumor I mean, the one about you selling the foundry to them."

Alejandro stared straight back into the other man's eyes, "None whatsoever."

"Well, now, that's good to hear."

"Trust me, we will not be selling."

"I will take you at your word, *jefe*. We all know that you are an *honest* man who would not lie; certainly, not about something that could have such an impact on the lives of those around you."

Alejandro looked at the man momentarily. Why such an emphasis on the word "honest"? What was he trying to say? Was there some hidden message in that statement? What did he know?

The chittering of the monkey distracted him and he looked back down into the pool of golden liquid that sat enticingly in the glass on the bar.

"Have a drink with me," Junior said and motioned for the bartender to give him shots of tequila.

"Thank you," Alejandro responded, "but I do not drink."

"You don't," Junior asked with a pointed look at the drink that sat in front of his boss.

Alejandro followed the other man's gaze and responded, "Sometimes, I come in and order one — only to look at. I never drink it."

"I see," Junior replied. "That's a little strange."

Alejandro shrugged. He hoped the movement might encourage the man to move his arm from his shoulder, but it did not.

For his part, Junior felt the old man's shrug as it jostled his arm. He could not help but hear the voice of Eldon from so long ago: *"Don't just shrug, boy,"* Eldon said, *"Use your words. Can't you communicate?"*

The memory of Eldon was a lightning strike in Junior's soul and he felt that strike erupt into flame. Who knows what he might have done had the bartender not interrupted and placed two shots in front of his patrons.

Junior looked down at the shots. He removed his arm from Alejandro's shoulder to push the drink toward him with his left hand.

To Alejandro, it seemed that the other man had moved with such deliberation to call his attention to the motion. When he looked down, he saw the glass of tequila in front of him and heard the monkey chittering again.

"Feed me!" the monkey cried. "Feed me! Feed me! Feed . . ."

The monkey's demand silenced when Alejandro noticed the hand that moved the glass. That hand was missing its three middle fingers.

He stared down at that man's hand and his eyes widened in surprise, then, quickly, he looked up and back into the other man's eyes. From behind those eyes, he saw *La Furia* lurking.

The man smiled at him, tossed another handful of peanuts into his mouth with his good hand, then leaned into Alejandro and whispered into his ear, "I will be seeing you again, *padrino*. Real soon," before the man turned and walked away.

CHAPTER 21

Junior followed the old man from the church.

This was an upper income neighborhood called Wrightwood Estates (named after its founder, Mr. John C. Wright). But it was often referred to by the locals as "Rightside" — maybe that was because these homes were deep on one side of the highway that split the town in half. Those on the other side of the highway, the side that was away from Wrightwood, were thought to have come from the "wrong side" of the tracks, thus, this was the "right side."

While this was a nice suburban, upscale area, it was by no means as posh as those areas that contained the homes of the upper echelons of society, but it was one that spoke to wealth — the kind of wealth that comes from owning a business rather than laboring for one.

With each passing block, the homes grew in size as did the lots on which they sat. White picket fences that surrounded manicured lawns gave way to stone ones with wrought iron spires evidencing the increasing wealth of the neighborhood.

Looking at these houses, Junior could not help but recall the early years of his own life; the years that he spent living in a two-room shack with dirt floors and no indoor plumbing. He recalled the many nights spent on those dirt floors and he felt a tingling in his belly.

The farther removed from the warehouses, yard and docks where he worked, the farther removed the occupants became from the ordinary people that populated the majority of this ordinary city; the people who worked within the businesses they owned.

Contemplating the lives of these people, these men and women of privilege, Junior recalled the ordinary lives of the ordinary people that he had known most of his life. Simple men and women who, like Emma and Eldon, were not caught up in the trappings of wealth. Good, ordinary folk who worked hard each and every day to make a good and ordinary life for themselves. The ordinary people who struggled to make a living, yet found joy in the ordinary, little things that life offered.

And as he thought on Emma and Eldon, his belly began to itch.

It struck Junior as more than a little odd that Hector now belonged to these upper reaches. Despite the man's education, were they both not from the very fields where the *gringos* ruled and the *braceros* served at their whim? How had Hector managed to climb from those desperate beginnings to become no different from the *gringo* masters that once he served? Was this because of some pact that he had made with the Devil himself some thirty years ago? When he murdered Mariana, shot Luciana, and took Junior's hand, was that the tithe he paid at the behest of the demon? Were Hector's current riches his reward for carrying out the will of Evil?

How was it that Junior had been unable to climb from those

depths and into a better life? Had Hector's compact with the Devil on that night some thirty years before imbued him with a Midas touch? Had Hector traded his soul for gold; that black gold that erupted from the Texas earth?

As he thought on these things, his belly began to burn.

When the old man turned down the driveway to a two-story Edwardian home, Junior stood at the end of that driveway and looked up to the house. There was so little moonlight that the shadows of the night hid his form from any unwanted attention as he watched Hector enter the home. Looking at the large house with its fancy environs, Junior, again, recalled the dirt-floor shack that held all of the members of his own family jammed within.

As he looked on that house, the heat in his belly rose.

Junior watched through the large plate-glass window at the front of the home. He assumed that the woman, although younger than Hector, must be the man's wife. He had heard talk around the yard that *el jefe* had married a younger woman and that he had a son. That progeny Junior knew to be in his twenties, now. He strained to see if the younger man was home.

Watching the old man laugh and talk with his wife, Junior's mind wandered backward in time to the nights of his youth. There was little laughter shared between his Papa Jesús and Mama Fabia. Junior recalled far more tears than he did merriment.

And the heat in his belly burned.

He recalled many nights that he accompanied his sister, Luciana, to the outhouse to guard over her as she did her business. He remembered those nights fondly; how they laughed at the moon and dreamed with the stars. He recalled and cherished the little jokes they shared as his sister stood over the stove stirring that old pot of beans, and the memory of the deep, rich chocolate that she hid in her bedding to share with him later. He almost smiled as he thought on these things; almost.

Then the memory of that terrible morning came flooding into his consciousness and he recalled watching in horror as his sister fell to the floor in a pool of crimson.

The flames of his memory licked at his mind in much the same way that the flames of the stove had once licked at his fingers.

He felt the burning in his non-existent fingers run up his arm to meet the burning in his chest that had risen from his belly.

As a boy, he lived like so many others in mere shacks overflowing with large families — like his very own. Thereafter, the only places he had to call home were temporary. There were those years near El Paso with Emma and Eldon, the surrogate parents who he had loved more than life itself. But those years had been too few and far too short before . . . well, before the burning that overtook his soul had also overtaken his home and he had been forced to move on. After they had been taken, the only "home," he had was whichever bunkhouse was offered at whatever job he held. His only "home" was wherever he found a place to lay his head — at least that was until he met Ginny.

It seemed so unjust, then, that Hector lived in a such a large home in this, the better part of town. It seemed wrong that after every-thing that Hector had done to Junior and to his family that he was rewarded with riches and respect.

"If only," he thought, "others knew the man Hector; if only they knew he had made a compact with the Devil; if only they knew the true man hidden within; if only they knew the monster that he was; if only . . ."

Hector had murdered Mariana! And, yet, here, the old man lived with another woman. Here, the old man lived and raised a family to call his own.

Hector had stolen Luciana's legs. Yet, here, he danced to the music of a good life.

Hector had stolen Junior's fingers, yet, the old man strummed the instrument of life with his own, unmarred hand.

As he considered these things from the edge of the driveway, Junior lit a cigarette and continued to spy. The flame of the match-stick inflamed the heat within him.

As he watched, the woman went upstairs, presumably to bed. Junior looked down at his watch and realized that he had been standing, rooted in this spot for almost two hours. While the woman made her way up the stairs, the old man did not.

Junior saw the light in one room go out while one in another came on. He moved closer on the driveway and to the left, deep into the garden, so that he could continue to watch his prey from a blind. That garden reminded him of the fields he once worked as a child, but the fruit this garden bore he knew was the fruit of evil.

Through the upstairs window, Junior clearly saw the woman make ready for bed.

"It won't be too much longer, now," he thought and lit another cigarette.

In the downstairs window, Junior watched as the old man pulled a bottle of liquor from a desk and poured a drink. He snorted in derision as he recalled the old man's words from earlier in the evening — "I don't drink," he had said.

"Another lie by a man who knows no truth," Junior thought as the flame in his belly blazed.

The upstairs window went dark, as the man downstairs retrieved paper from his desk. The urge to go in now almost overtook him, but he knew that he had to wait. He could do nothing until the woman was soundly asleep. He had no beef with her, after all.

He watched as the old man put pen to paper and thought on all the injustice of his life. For what seemed an eternity, but in fact was mere minutes, he stood motionless, and surveilled the old man through the window until his vision began to blur. With his right hand, he reached up to clutch his forehead to quench the piercing pain that invaded his skull.

The blazing inferno that had begun in his belly now engulfed him, and his body moved forward, but not of his own volition. Like Hector so many years before, Junior lost control while something else drove the chassis of his soul. From outside of himself, he watched as the thing that controlled him steered him toward the front doorway.

La Furia was in charge.

CHAPTER 22

"Are you coming up to bed?" Carmen asked.

"In a bit," he responded. "I have some business to tend to first."

"Well, don't be too late. You know how you can get in the morning when you have not had enough sleep."

Alejandro smiled at his wife who came to his side and kissed him gently on his cheek. "Sleep well," he said to her.

"Good night," and she walked out of the den and up the stairs.

He watched his wife walk up those stairs and marveled at what a lucky man he had been these past many years. Despite all of the trials and tribulations that he had faced, he had come through the other end a better man than the one that he had left behind. Whether that betterment was due to his own grappling with demons that he overcame or the influence of this wonderful woman, he did not know.

Confessing to his priest had not relieved him of remorse any more than the prayers he made were sufficient penance to atone for those sins, and he knew what he must do. His eyes watered with the tears of tortured guilt.

It had been some thirty years since that morning in Arizona; thirty years of running and hiding from the monster that chased him. But now his past had caught up to him and the monster was at his gate. There was nowhere left to run. Nowhere left to hide. It was time to face the music.

"Long past time," he thought. Besides, he was an old man now. Even if he wanted to run away, there was nowhere to go. Nowhere that his past would not finally catch up to him. Nowhere that he could go to put the monster down once and for all.

Having made his confession, he knew that he owed his family some sort of explanation before he turned himself into the police that next morning. Maybe the past thirty years of a good and decent life would buy him some mercy from the court, but despite his riches, he was not at all certain that he had the coin.

Alejandro reached into the bottom drawer of his antique, mahogany desk, and pulled out the brown paper bag that contained the liquid courage he had purchased earlier in the evening. He blew the dust from his coffee cup, then extracted the bottle of whiskey from the bag.

It had been so many years since he last had a drink, but he knew that tonight was the night to do so, if ever there was one. The chittering of the monkey demanded it and, for once, he would accede to its demands. He needed the strength that it promised if he were to fight the demon; if he were to find the courage to do what must be done.

He downed the first drink from his cup, grimaced, then poured another. From one of the desk drawers, he pulled out stationery and a pen. He wrote.

My Dearest Carmen,

By the time that you read this letter, I will have already been arrested and likely locked in a cell in the police station. I cannot begin to tell you how sorry I am for what I know will be a difficult time for you and our son.

For years, I have lived with the guilt and shame of what a man has done. A man that only now can be named.

There are so many things that you will hear over the course of the next few days and months, things that will make you come to understand the evil that I have wrought. Don't let those things diminish your love for me. The things that you learn were not done by the man that you know. They were done by the man that I left behind. A man that you never knew and that I had hoped and prayed you never would come to know. But the sins of a man cannot be erased. They can only be forgiven when that man accepts responsibility for them. It is long past the time that I do so.

I have already confessed my sins to God and Father Tom. Show him this letter so that he knows that he has my permission to tell you everything that I have told him. I would tell you myself, but the truth is, I do not have the courage to tell you on my own. The thought of seeing the esteem you hold for me drain from your eyes is far more than I could bear.

Know that you have made me a very happy man. These last twenty years have been far more than any single man could wish for; far more than any man deserves, certainly, far more than one such as I.

Know that, no matter what you may think of me after you learn the truth, I have loved you. That part of my life has never been a lie. My love for you has been deep and abiding since the first moment that I laid eyes upon you; since that time that you walked into that bar in Midland and greeted your husband. Regardless of what happens now or in the future, that will never change. My love for you will remain no matter where I am or what becomes of me.

In time, I hope that you can learn to forgive me for all of the lies that I have told. In time, I hope that you will find another to make you happy — at least as happy as you have made me.

All my love,

Alex

When he was done, he read the letter, then carefully folded it and inserted it into an envelope which he addressed to "*Mi Carina.*" He set the letter aside and sat back in his chair folding his hands in front of him, before sitting forward and pouring another drink from the bottle of whiskey.

From outside of the window, he thought he saw a shadowy figure in the garden. He looked out more intently, but saw nothing. Turning back to his desk, he pulled out a fresh sheet of paper and began writing his second missive.

My son,

I know that you must be confused by all that is happening. I wanted for you to hear this from me, before the word got out and you started to hear all of the stories from other people — before you found out the truth from another. So, this is my confession to you:

Thirty years ago, I killed my wife.

In the days long before I met your mother, long before I hit oil in the fields near Midland, and long before I started this business that now will become yours, I was a different man. When I say that I was a different man, I am being true and sincere. Alejandro Melendez did not exist. Back then, I was known as Hector Rivera.

While I was Hector, I worked harvesting the fields for ranchers from Texas to Arizona and sometimes beyond. I crossed the Rio Grande somewhere near Edinburg to work those fields with my wife, Mariana.

Yes, my son, this is but one of the secrets that I have carried these many years. I was married before your mother. She knows nothing of my past. The only person that I have told is Father Tom and now you, as I confess in this letter.

A noise from outside the window interrupted his train of thought and Alejandro, the man who once was Hector, looked out the window again. Seeing nothing, he turned back to the paper in front of him.

For years, Mariana and I lived the life of migrant workers. We moved from ranch to ranch picking whatever was in season. I had a degree from Universidad de Mexico, that much of my past is true, but that paper meant nothing here in the States. So, we did what we had to do to make ends meet.

It was a hard life, but it was not a bad one. Even though she could not give me the child I wanted, I was in love with my wife, and we had resigned ourselves to being childless. Maybe that is why when my friend, Jesús, asked us to become padrinos to his children, we so readily agreed.

At the time, Mariana and I were very close to Jesús and his wife. And we became even closer with each new child that we sponsored into the Church. In many ways, those children were like my own.

He thought that he saw movement across the window pane and the old man looked up from his task again. He cocked his head toward that window and strained to see through the shadows. For a full minute, he stared out that window, but stared at nothing.

By now, you have heard the story of who I am and what I have done. You know that one day, I found that my Mariana had been sleeping with Jesús. On that day, I snapped. Anger and fury overtook me and drove me to do the unthinkable. In a fit of rage and with vengeance in my heart, I killed my sweet Mariana and then went after Jesús. But I was not successful in killing my friend. Instead, I only succeeded in hurting his children, Luciana and Junior.

Because of my actions, since that day, Luciana has been unable to walk. I do not know where she is or what has become of her at this time, but if you can, please find her. Tell her that I am sorry for what I have done. I have enclosed a check with this letter. Deliver it to her. Perhaps, it may ease her suffering.

The old man thought he saw a flash of light outside the window but when he looked up, again, he saw nothing.

On that morning, Junior was grievously injured. Unlike Luciana, I do know what became of him.

I first learned of his whereabouts again in Midland. That is what spurred us to move here all of those years ago. You were young, but old enough to remember that move. That was the second time that I ran away. I knew that Junior was looking for me. I knew that he intended to get payback for what I had done. But even then, I could not tell your mother about it. And I certainly could not tell you — you were only a little boy, back then. I had hoped that in the distance, Junior would lose track of me. But no matter how far a man runs, he cannot outrun his past.

Alejandro (or was it Hector again? The old man was confused and uncertain who he was as he put his confession to paper) saw another flash of light from outside his window.

He stood and moved to the window looking into the garden. He thought that he saw a form, the shadowy figure of someone standing just at the hedges that formed the boundary between his property and the street, but he could not be certain. He felt a tingle run down his spine when, from behind the still form, he saw the shadow of great wings rise high above what must have been the figure's head.

"She has found me," he thought. "All that I ask for is a little more time to complete my confession."

He turned and walked back to his desk. Pouring himself another drink, then took a sip and returned to the paper in front of him.

> Junior is now a man and he works at the foundry. If you ask around, you will find him. Ask the men to point out the one with the missing three fingers on his left hand. That is the man who once was the boy, Junior. That is the man that I saw tonight on my way home. When I saw him, I knew that I could no longer outrun my past. So, I confessed my sins to Father Tom. By the time that you read this letter, I will already be at the police station confessing to them.

Glancing back at the window, he thought he saw the shadow move from its position at the edge of the garden to one much closer to the house.

"I don't have much time," he thought, "I must finish. Dear God," he prayed, "give me the time to complete this task."

> I know that you must be very confused and more than a little angry with me. For that, I am truly sorry. I had hoped that this day would never come, but it has. They say that the truth will always come out in the end. The only surprise is that it has taken so long for the past to catch up to me.

I have always regretted the sins of my past, more than you can possibly know. I prayed to God that those sins would never affect you or your mother in any way. It is still my hope and prayer that this is true and that the monster that has chased me down does not visit its wrath on you. I hope that, in time, you may come to understand and forgive me even as I cannot forgive myself.

Take care of your mother. She will need you in the upcoming times.

What is there to say that you have not already heard a thousand times over? You are my pride and joy. You are my son and I love you more than a father has any right to love his son.

Your father,

Alejandro

Having finished this letter, Alejandro read, folded the letter and inserted it into an envelope which he addressed to "My Son".

He poured himself another drink, stood and walked to the window. The shadow that he had seen before was no longer there. He did not know where it had gone, but he felt his heart drop at its absence.

Returning to his desk, he started his final letter.

Dear Junior,

How can I begin to express the regret that I feel? You did not deserve the torment that you have endured. That such torment derived from the actions of your very own padrino sickens me. It was my job to take care of you and your brothers and sisters. I am so very sorry that I failed so miserably in doing so.

For many, many years, I have wondered what became of you and your sister, Luciana. But my guilt and my shame prevented me from searching. And yes, as long as I am confessing, let me say that it is not only that guilt and shame that prevented me from finding you, but also my own need for self-preservation. I was afraid. I was afraid to go to jail and afraid to lose everything that I have spent thirty years building; my business, my reputation, the goodwill of my community, my wife, and my family. The fear of losing all of that prevented me from ever seeking you out to express my sorrow over what I had done. But I guess that loss cannot compare to what you have lost — what I have taken from you.

For the last thirty years, I have been looking over my shoulder wondering when that past might catch up to me.

I first knew of you as a man when you came to Midland. But I was afraid and ran away. I should have known that fate would eventually bring you back to me here and now. The Devil must have his due after all, and I am ready to pay for my sins.

Do what you must, but in the end, forgive yourself even if you cannot forgive me.

It seems so strange to sign this name again after so long.

Your padrino,

Hector

Now finished with his third and final letter, Alejandro addressed the envelope to Junior. These three letters he tucked within the pages of the large checkbook that he stored in the center drawer of the desk. This was the place that he knew his family would find them; not immediately, but in time and when necessary.

He downed the rest of the drink from his cup, then reached over and poured another. He leaned back in his chair holding that drink in one hand wondering: Had he said enough? Would they understand?

From behind him, he heard a noise. He did not turn. He knew the sound of *La Furia's* footsteps.

"'I've been expecting you," he said with back still turned on the monster. Then, he felt a sharp pain to the side of his head and fell from the chair onto the floor. Dazed and confused, he looked up, and saw the mark of *La Furia* move toward him before the darkness overtook his vision.

Sitting in the small hospital room, holding her husband's hand, she repeated the mantra, "Open your eyes. Open your eyes. Open your eyes."

Her own eyes, although open, were swollen and red from the tears that she had shed the last forty-eight hours. She was tired from the lack of sleep. Although the room was private, it was not a comfortable place for rest.

"Open your eyes," she whispered to him again ignoring the sting in her own.

Sniffling, she looked down at her husband. His left hand was bandaged. It would heal, the doctors had said, but the missing fingers could not be reattached. Too much time had passed between their severing and delivery to the hospital and they were too mutilated to save. That they had managed to find the fingers at the bottom of the trash can, hidden beneath the bottle of whiskey and other rubbish was miracle enough. To expect that miracle to extend to a successful reattachment was more than could be hoped for.

The ventilator that protruded from his mouth was white and taped down to the sides of his face. This instrument was the only thing that kept Alejandro breathing.

His spine had been severed at C-5, but the doctors believed that he might yet breathe on his own. However, even if he finally woke from his coma, he would remain paralyzed from the neck down, forever more unlikely to move any other muscle below his shoulders.

CHAPTER 23

"Helluva day," Michael, Alejandro's son, thought as he pulled out of the hospital parking lot and turned onto the street that would eventually lead him to I-10 and then home.

Neither Michael nor his mother had left Alejandro's side since finding his father lying in a pool of blood. He was tired and he reeked. He needed a bath. He needed some sleep. But most of all, he needed to know what the hell had happened!

Like any normal twenty-three-year-old, he had gone out the night before with some of his friends. They were in celebration mode. This was the last year of school and there were but a few short weeks remaining until the end of the term; the end of his under-grad days.

Since he and his girlfriend had broken-up over Christmas, he was anxiously looking forward to going out and meeting someone new. He was anticipating the start of his graduate studies in the fall, this next chapter of his life that would begin after this term, after the summer. But he did not want to think about that. He wanted to think about partying the night away and having a good time.

He did not get in until very late that night, or rather, in the wee hours of the next morning. It was about 3:30 a.m. when finally he had pulled into the driveway then entered the home.

"I should have known!" he berated himself. "I should have seen that something was wrong!"

But he had not. The house was quiet as a church mouse, but that was not unusual for that time of night. How many nights had he quietly slipped into the house, up the stairs and into his bedroom without being noticed by his sleeping parents? Each time he had done this in the past, the house had been just as quiet, just as dark. There was no reason to suspect that anything was amiss. How could he have known?

To himself, he thought, "I should have checked. I should have looked in the office. If I had checked, I would have found him so much earlier. We could have gotten him to the hospital sooner. We could have called the police earlier. Something, anything, that might have been done in that short window of time might have changed what was happening now!"

Michael despaired over the current situation — his father in a hospital bed, unable to move, fingers sliced off by some madman that snuck into the house while his mother slept and Michael was out — partying.

"Dammit!" he thought. "I should not have gone out at all. I should have stayed home. None of this would have happened if I had just stayed home."

The cynical part of his mind, the part that always contradicted him, retorted its own observation, "What would you have done?" it asked. "How would you have stopped a monster?"

But the reptilian part of his brain, the part formally known as the amygdala, rejected the observations of his cynical neo-cortex. The reptilian part, the part that ruled anger and violence retorted, "I would have kicked his ass; that's what I would have done! I would have saved my father from this humiliation."

But even as this inner debate continued in his mind, there was another part of his brain, that part that knew, there was likely nothing that he could have done.

The monster that invaded their home and so grievously injured Michael's father was smart. It had waited until his mother had gone to bed. It waited long enough to know that she was deep in slumber and would not hear him as he mutilated her husband. That monster would surely have made certain that Michael, too, was safely off to the Land of Nod before carrying out its nefarious plan. Michael, like his mother, would have slept through the entire ordeal that the husband and father must have endured in the office on the first floor of their home. If he had not, even if he had interrupted the monster's work, if truth be told, the monster would likely only have overpowered him, and then devoured them both.

Throughout this internal debate about what he "coulda, woulda, or shoulda" done, Michael continued his drive home. He was so tired that he may have fallen asleep at the wheel, had it not been for the adrenaline that coursed through his system; an adrenaline that began pumping from the moment he saw his father lying on the floor.

Thoughts of those early hours invaded his mind.

Michael was dreaming of the tow-haired girl he saw at the bar, the one in the short skirt and a bow in her hair. This was the girl that, despite his having spent hours flirting with her and countless dollars on drinks, ultimately rebuffed his advances. But in his dreams, she could not, and would not, reject him.

Just as his dreams were turning to the good part, the part that he would clearly remember in the morning when he pictured her face in the shower, he was startled awake by a scream.

"Aaaaaiiiiieeeee!" The sound was so loud and so piercing that Michael sat bolt upright in bed. From the floor below he heard, "Noooooooo! Alejandro!" and more wails from his mother.

Michael jumped from his bed and tripped over the pair of sneakers that he had haphazardly tossed on the floor when he undressed for bed. He righted himself and bound down the stairs two at a time.

He slid into the open doorway to the office and saw his mother on the floor over his father's prone body.

For her part, Carmen looked up at her son and noted that he wore only his boxers, the blue ones that had the rip on the side. For the tiniest of moments, she thought to herself, "He needs new underwear," before her mind brought her back screeching to reality.

"Call 9-1-1," she said to her son.

"What happened?" he asked.

"Just call 9-1-1 now!"

Michael ran to the desk and picked up the phone. Holding the cordless hand-piece, he punched in the numbers.

"9-1-1, what is your emergency?" he heard from the other end of the line, but he could not answer. His voice caught in his throat as he looked down at his father's mutilated hand and the blood (so much blood!) on the floor beneath the man.

"Hello? 9-1-1," the voice on the other end of the line said through the earpiece.

But Michael's voice remained stayed as he looked into his father's eyes; eyes that were open and staring at him although no other part of him stirred.

"9-1-1. What's your emergency?" he heard through the line again and this time, the sound broke the spell.

"Yes, yes, sorry," he spoke into the phone turning away to avert his eyes from his father. "My father's been . . . attacked."

"Police or ambulance?"

"Both, dammit! Hurry!"

"Calm down, sir. Help is on the way. I have your address as . . ."

The call continued for a few short minutes until Michael heard the sounds of sirens grow louder and louder as they approached his home. His mother had wrapped Alejandro's hand in a towel. Over her sobs, she tried to comfort her motionless husband.

"It's ok," she said. "They are coming. They are almost here. It'll be ok."

Michael turned onto his street and drove six houses down, into the driveway of the family home. He parked the car and exited. In his weariness, he almost dropped his keys to the ground but managed to hold on to them.

When he approached the front door, he spied the torn, yellow tape that repeated the words "Crime Scene Do Not Enter" over and over across its span.

Michael felt a tingle in his belly, a rising anger at . . . he didn't know what, but a rising anger all the same. Perhaps, it was anger at the situation as a whole. Perhaps, he would never know. He took his anger out on that tape.

"Fuck 'em," he said to himself as he reached up and tore the yellow tape from the door.

"This is *my* house," he thought, "and I will enter as I please."

Besides, he knew that the police had already searched the home and came up empty of clues. They did not know who the perpetrator of this crime was, but they promised that they would find out.

"Imbeciles," he thought and entered the home.

He stopped within a few feet of the doorway and turned to look at the office. From where he stood, he clearly saw the congealed blood on the office floor. At the sight, he felt a burning in his belly.

He started toward the office, then stopped. He was not yet ready to face that devastation. He turned away then slowly trudged up the stairs, down the hall, through his room, into the adjoining bathroom. He stripped himself of his clothing, the very same clothing that he had worn these last forty-eight hours. As he did so, he noticed the little rip in his blue boxers.

"I need some new ones," he thought before he violently threw them into the wastebasket next to the toilet.

Michael let the hot water knead his neck and shoulders as he cleansed himself. But all the while, he thought and wondered.

"Why would anyone do this to my father?" and as he thought this, the heat in his belly ignited.

"He is an honorable and respected man. Everyone loves him. He gives so much to everyone. He gives money to charity. He is generous with his employees," and the heat in his belly burned.

"What kind of a sick individual would brutalize an old man that way? What kind of person would do that to another human being?" and the flame in his belly grew.

Through gritted teeth, aloud he said, "More importantly, who?"

Burning with an anger that bordered on rage, Michael finished his shower then dressed and purposefully walked down the stairs.

"The police may not have found anything," he thought, "but I will."

He stopped at the doorway to the office looking into the room. For a full minute, he stood there as his eyes passed over every piece of furniture, every item atop that furniture, every corner, and every nook and cranny, before he finally crossed the threshold into that room.

The fire in his belly burned bright but there was nothing for it to consume. There was no place or no one toward whom the flame could be directed. Michael searched that room looking for something, anything that might lead him to the monster.

When he was almost ready to surrender the search, he opened the large checkbook that sat in the center drawer and there, between two of its pages, he saw the letters.

CHAPTER 24

Ginny had never seen her husband so happy. He had come in late the other night and she knew that he had been out with "the boys" likely having more than his fair share of spirits. She didn't much care that he sometimes drank, but that drinking was never in excess and he always came home at night. Wasn't that the most important thing — that, in the end, he always returned to her?

But given that he returned so late, she assumed that he had seriously tied one on. Yet, this entire weekend, he seemed perfectly fine, as if he had never had better rest. He was more jocular and lighter than she had ever seen him. Where once he seemed to carry the very weight of the world on his shoulders, that burden now was lifted.

She could not help but wonder, "Why? Why has he been this way for the last two or three days?" and she did not know what to make of it.

Junior's mood was infectious, though. She, too, felt lighthearted. She smiled at him and laughed at his jokes; giggling like a schoolgirl who had only just met her teen idol crush. She shook her head. This was nothing like her. She was not some empty-headed, little girl! Still, the butterflies in her stomach would not stop and she hummed a little song as she puttered around the kitchen.

After pouring a cup of coffee, she leaned against the door jamb between the kitchen and living room watching her husband play with their son, Jessie.

The child was ten-years old and he was the perfect blend of the two of them. He had the striking good looks of his father and the keen and insightful mind of his mother. The boy had the sunniest of dispositions. Even as a baby, he rarely cried and as he grew, he was the kind of child that any mother would love to have. Rarely, did Ginny find herself having to discipline the boy as he had a natural affinity to always do the right thing. He was a very mature and responsible ten-year old.

She wondered whether the commingling of genetic material had ever made such a perfect child? Watching her family, she could not help but grin from ear to ear.

"I am going to make breakfast," she said. "What do ya'll want?"

Junior looked up from his play with his son and smiled that smile that always made her swoon.

"Let's go out for breakfast," he said.

"Go out?" she asked and looked at her husband askance.

This was new. He never wanted to go out to eat. He always said: "Why waste money paying someone to do what you can do for yourself?" This was not at all like him; not at all.

"Yeah," he replied. "Today is a special day and I want to do something special for you, for Jessie, for us."

"What makes today so special?" she asked.

Junior turned away from her and looked back at his son. "Because we are alive, and all is right in the world," he said, then began to tickle his son's ribs as the boy squealed in delight.

Ginny looked at her husband feeling mildly alarmed and wondered, "What in the world has gotten into him?" Despite the alarm, she could not help but smile as she watched her two favorite boys play on the living room floor.

Shaking her head, she asked, "Who are you? And what have you done with my husband?"

Through laughter, Junior responded, "It's a good day and I'm feeling great. I want my two favorite people in the world to feel as good as I do."

Ginny cocked her head toward her husband wearing a smirk. She shrugged her shoulder and said, "Well, I guess we better get dressed then."

"Yes, ma'am," her husband replied. "Now, go on upstairs and make yourself look 'purty' for me."

"Aye, Aye, captain," she responded and turned toward the staircase that led up to the second floor.

"You too, *mocoso*," Junior said to his son. "Are you hungry? Let's go get dressed!"

The child laughed and stood to scamper up the stairs.

As Junior rose to follow, the doorbell rang.

Ginny, halfway up the stairs, called down, "Would you get that?"

"Your wish is my command," Junior replied and turned toward the door.

Ginny continued up the stairs and into her bedroom to change. The child, Jessie, curious to see who was at the door this Sunday morning, waited halfway up the staircase and watched his father open the door.

As Junior moved toward the door, he imagined how it would go down.

The policemen may, or may not, have weapons drawn. But, that didn't really matter, did it? He had no intention of resisting.

He had watched the scene play out on television enough times to know that the cops would read him his rights — probably while they handcuffed him.

They would walk him out to the waiting patrol car and one would place a hand on his head as he bent to sit in the backseat of that vehicle while Ginny and Jessie watched from the doorway confused, not understanding what was happening. Junior's only regret would be that they did not make it to breakfast that morning.

There would be several police there. Some with the intent to search the house and look for evidence of a crime. Of course, they would find none. Junior was not stupid enough to leave any kind of evidence in the house. There was nothing that they might find that would definitively link him to any crime; nothing at all.

He imagined that there would be two cops in the car that drove him to the police station. One would be short with a bulbous nose. He would be the surly hardass. The other would be tall and lanky. Naturally, he would play good cop.

They would interrogate him for hours trying to find a crack in his story; something that they could exploit and use against him; something they could find that would definitively point to his guilt. But, they would get nothing out of him. He had heard those rights they had read to him. He would not say a word until his lawyer arrived and that lawyer would cogently argue for his release.

Finally, unable to find sufficient evidence to hold him, they would be forced to set him free. Then he would have to explain to Ginny. He prayed that she would believe his lie, or, if he decided to tell her the truth, that she might understand.

If, by some miracle, they did find enough evidence to try him, he would be forthright and honest about it all. There was no way that he would lie to the jury. If he stood accused of a crime and had to face twelve of his peers, he would tell them the truth, the whole truth, and nothing but the truth, so help him God. The jury would be sure to empathize once they heard that truth.

In his mind, he pictured himself dressed in his Sunday-best and hand-in-hand with his wife walking into the courthouse. As they approached the courthouse steps, he would see a small crowd gathered outside and the sheriff's deputies that duly held them back. Members of that crowd, people who had loved Alejandro (not Hector, he reminded himself — these people had never known that monster) would hold signs and call out demands for his death.

In the lead-up to the trial, he imagined that Alejandro's friends and family might harass and harangue him. He and Ginny would consider moving, but would not do so, knowing that the mob would find them sooner or later. It would do no good. A man cannot outrun his past. He cannot escape his sins, after all. Despite the well-deserved justification, Junior did not try to fool himself into believing that he had committed no sin. His action was not right, but neither was it wrong.

He imagined that the local news would run constant coverage about this local man's death. Newspaper editorials would ennoble Alejandro, not knowing that the man they praised was not the same man who had been injured. Concurrently, they would refer to Junior as a monster without remorse. A monster that must be banished from their borders.

Of course, they could not understand. They did not know of the terrible things that Hector had done when Junior was but a child. They did not know about Mariana. They did not know what had happened to Luciana. They did not know that it was the man named Hector who had been wearing the guise of Alejandro, that great philanthropist and beloved citizen of their town. They did not know who Alejandro truly was. They did not know that Hector was the real monster.

But in his own mind, Junior also knew that would change. He imagined that he had persuaded Mama Fabia to bring Luciana to the trial, and that his sister was set to testify on his behalf. Thereafter, each and every one of these protestors would learn the truth.

They would learn about the murder and mayhem that Hector had caused. They would learn the heartbreaking tale of Luciana. They would learn of his own misfortune; the loss of his fingers.

Oh, they would learn. They would learn it all.

They would discover who the true monster was, and even if Junior was convicted for Alejandro's attack, he could go to the "Walls Unit" (that infamous penitentiary in Huntsville) comforted by the knowledge that the curtain had finally been revealed. The world would know about "Alejandro Melendez's" lies.

If need be, he would happily go to his death, if that is what a jury determined, secure in the knowledge that Hector could do no harm. No other woman would be murdered; no other child would live paralyzed or grow up without their fingers because of the actions of this man, Hector. That evil had been excised.

Secure in the knowledge that he had slain the monster, Junior would gladly watch the door of that prison close.

CHAPTER 25

Beyond the door, Michael clearly heard the sounds from within as he stood at the threshold of the monster's lair.

The monster was playing (actually playing!) with a child on the floor. That monster was laughing, acting for all the world as if nothing was amiss. The giggles of the child were almost more than Michael could bear. Did the child not know that he was playing with a monster?

From deeper within the house, Michael heard the sound of a woman's voice. "The monster's mate?" he wondered. Was she as evil as he? Was the child the spawn of the monster? Would that child be a monster too?

The conversation within the home turned to breakfast. Breakfast! How could the monster even consider eating after what he had done? How could that loathsome creature be so nonchalant in the face of the tragedy that he had wrought?

Michael moved closer to the door and strained to hear more of the conversation, but most of what he heard emanating from within were muffled sounds. Were they the sounds of the monster's evil or were they only the sounds of a normal family?

For a moment, he stopped himself. He recalled the letters that his father had written. He had read each — not only the one addressed to him. It was through those letters that he came to know the secret identity of the monster within this house.

But doubt crept into his mind. It was a doubt that was unyielding. He recalled the words of his father, the words the man had written to his mother: *"For years I have lived with the guilt and shame of what a man has done. A man that only now can be named."*

Was it right to blame the man behind the door? After all, his father was not the man Michael thought he knew. His father was in fact, *". . . the man that I left behind. A man that you never knew and that I had hoped and prayed you never would come to know."*

If his father was not the man he claimed to be, could he, Michael, blame the one inside the house for what he had done?

But what did he do exactly? Michael recalled the words his father had written to him: *". . . this is my confession to you: Thirty years ago, I killed my wife."*

Could it be? Was it possible that his own father was, in fact, the real monster here? After all, if, as his father had written, *"Alejandro Melendez did not exist. Back then, I was called Hector Rivera"* how could Michael know who the real man was — or who was the real monster?

His father confessed in that letter that he had *". . . killed my sweet Mariana and then went after Jesús."* His father was a murderer — if the old man's letter was to be believed.

And, still, there was more: *"But I was not successful in killing my* friend. Instead, I only succeeded in hurting his children, Luciana and Junior."*

The man across the threshold, this man, 'Junior', was he justified in his actions? Perhaps, Junior was not the monster at all, but a victim of some other demon. Would two monsters battle each other? If they did, how does one choose which monster to support?

Michael swooned at the thoughts in his head and the implication in his father's letters. At the door, he bent with hands on his knees. He began to feel nauseated, lightheaded, and weak. He needed to sit.

The words in the letter came back to him: *"Junior is now a man and he works at the foundry. If you ask around, you will find him. Ask the men to point out the one with the missing three fingers on his left hand."*

Junior had not been difficult to find after he read that letter. All that he had to do was go down to the foundry and look at the man's personnel file. Nobody would deny him. He was the son of the great Alejandro Melendez — the owner of the plant. He was Alejandro's rightful heir, after all, and soon, he would rule this kingdom.

Right there, in black ink, was the man's address.

But the final letter, the one that Michael's father had written to Junior, that was the letter that freed Michael of any doubts as to who was the perpetrator of his father's injuries. That letter said all that needed to be said.

His father wrote: *"For the last thirty years, I have been looking over my shoulder wondering when that past might catch up to me. . . I should have known that fate would eventually bring you back to me here and*

now. The Devil must have his due after all, and I am ready to pay for
my sins. Do what you must."

There could be no doubt that this man, Junior, was the perpetrator
of the horrible crime that had been committed against Michael's
father. Junior was the one who had committed the crime. Junior
was the monster.

For that, Michael knew, Junior must pay.

Michael heard the giggling from within the home and the fire in
his belly rose again. The sounds of the cheerful laughter stoked
those flames. The anger and fury continued to build as he listened
in.

What difference did it make if his father had done something
wrong thirty years ago, long before Michael was even born, before
Michael was even a glint in the old man's eyes? Who cared if the
man called Hector had done some horrific thing? That man,
Hector, that was not Michael's father. No! Michael's father was
Alejandro and that man, Alejandro, was a good and decent man
who had done nothing to deserve the barbarity that the monster,
Junior, had inflicted upon him.

He shook his head to clear his thoughts as he stood at the door to
the house. Junior was evil. Junior was a demon. Junior was the
monster!

As these thoughts coursed through his mind, the flame in his belly
grew larger until they cracked his soul. Through that fissure,
entered *La Furia*.

The demon that now controlled Michael's body reached up and
rang the doorbell.

CHAPTER 26

The child, Jessie, curious to see who was at the threshold this morning, waited halfway up the staircase and watched his father open the door.

It had been a fun morning. One of the best that he had ever had. His father was laughing and smiling in ways that the boy had never seen before.

He loved his father more than anything in the world! His father took care of him. Dad (not Daddy — he was too old to call him Daddy anymore) always made sure that there was food on the table for him to eat. Dad always made sure that he did his homework and said his prayers. Dad let him watch his favorite television shows and watched them with him, even when the boy knew that his father did not like the show. Dad did this, because that is what father's do. They sacrifice so that their children might experience glee. He watched those shows that he otherwise did not like so that his child could have that joy.

It was true that Dad sometimes disciplined him. But never in a mean or cruel way; never in the way that he knew some of his friends at school were punished. No, not his Dad. When his father disciplined him, the man made sure that Jessie understood why he was being punished, and that punishment was meant to teach him to be better. Not that he ever did anything that warranted discipline. He was a good boy, after all, and his daddy (Dad! He corrected himself) his Dad knew what a good boy he was. And Dad was a good father. He was the kind of man that would do whatever he had to ensure that his son was well cared for and happy. Jessie was, indeed, happy. How could he not be? He had the perfect family, the perfect mom, and the perfect dad.

He did well in school and was liked by each and every boy and girl there. His teachers gushed about how bright and imaginative he was. Like that time that Mrs. Cotter got angry with the entire class and told them to write a paper saying why they hated her so much. Jessie could not think of anything to say (even as other kids furiously wrote on the paper) and, instead, put his head down on the desk in tears. That is until she came over to him and whispered into his ear that he did not need to do the assignment. She knew that he was a good boy, too.

Jessie knew that he had a good life — the best life. This morning only proved that. Dad had been in such a happy mood. They had spent most of the morning wrestling around in the living room, talking, and laughing while his mother watched on. What more could he want? What more could any boy want?

When Dad suggested that they go out for breakfast, Jessie was ecstatic. What a rare treat to be able to go out for breakfast with his family! They would go to the little diner down the road and he would sit there, displaying only his best manners so as to impress the waitress and make Dad and Mom beam with pride when she complimented him. And he knew what he would order to eat too! He would have his favorite meal: *frijoles taquitos*. That had always been his favorite as far back as he could remember. All the way back to when he was still a little kid.

Wearing a large smile, he sat down on the stairs and watched as his father opened the door.

Junior opened the door not knowing what he would find, but half expecting to see policemen standing there. Nonetheless, he was feeling good, and he wore a bright smile as he did so. Even if the police were here to arrest him, he thought, well, then, so be it. He would take a beating so that the world might be free of a monster.

But there were no policemen. As he swung the door inward and looked through the opened doorway, all he saw was the flash of a gun's muzzle.

He heard the bang-bang-bang of three shots and felt the impact to his chest each time. Each new bang threw him back one more step until, finally, he tripped onto the coffee table that broke under his weight as he crashed into it.

He looked up as the man with the gun entered the home and pointed the weapon at his head. He heard his son, Jessie, jump down the stairs and the pitter-patter sound that the boy's feet made as he ran toward his father. He wanted to cry out, to tell his son to run the other way, but no words escaped his lips.

He looked from the barrel of the gun into the face of the man that had just shot him and then into that man's familiar eyes. He was the spitting image of his father. There was no doubt about this man's lineage. But there was something altogether different in those eyes. These were not the eyes of Hector's child looking down at him. These were the eyes of a monster. Junior knew only one way to evict that monster.

Through the gurgle of blood that began to drip from his open mouth, Junior whispered, "There ain't no monsters, except for the ones that we make."

He heard the retort of another bullet leaving the barrel of the gun before all went black.

Wearing a large smile, Jessie sat down on the stairs and watched as his father opened the door.

He heard the monster roar three times and felt a black tumor of fear emerge in his belly. As he watched his father fall to the floor, that tumor split and broke into two. The smaller part of the tumor changed from black to red and Jessie felt the heat begin to rise. It was a heat borne on the wings of anger. It was a rage that the child had never before experienced. It was complete and total, and it consumed him.

When the monster entered the home, the rage turned into fury. Without knowing what he was doing he felt that fury drive his body. He jumped from the steps almost tripping on the bottom one before catching himself. He ran toward the monster, but the monster did not see him as it roared once more and the boy's father's eye exploded in his head.

Jessie threw himself against the monster beating at the beast's torso and driving him back toward the door.

He watched himself from afar and heard his voice cry out, "Stay away from Daddy!" and pushed the monster back again almost knocking it off balance. His body, the very one that he no longer controlled, threw itself atop his father's and turned back to the monster staring him down. Daring that monster to come again.

He saw the monster's eyes widen in surprise.

From somewhere far away, Michael watched as his own hand, the hand he no longer controlled, the hand that was controlled by a demon, raise the gun and fire, reaping vengeance on his behalf.

He watched as Junior fell back into a coffee table that splintered under the crush of his weight.

He heard the cries from the steps of the stairwell, but did not see the boy run toward him as *La Furia* used his very own hand to once again raise the gun and point it at Junior's face. He watched his hand as the demon that controlled him pulled the trigger and, then in horror, as the man's eye exploded.

He barely felt the blows of the child's tiny fists as they pushed him back toward the door. When the child threw his body across that of his father, the child looked back at him with hate in his eyes.

He wanted to shout, "No! It's not my fault! It wasn't me. I swear that I did not do this! It was the monster; the demon that had taken control; the one that had driven my body!" but no words passed his lips.

As Michael looked on, he saw the shadow that was *La Furia* leave his body and watched in horror as it dove into the body of the little boy and for the tiniest of moments, Michael swore that he saw a smile emerge on the child's face.

EPILOGUE

There was no doubt about it; the man was evil — deserving of the death penalty. The man had no compassion for his victim, no kindness for those around him. Had it gone to trial, the jury most assuredly would have returned a guilty verdict. But no such verdict was made. No sentence was ever issued or carried out. The son of the victim had other plans, and before the man could face the consequences of his actions took justice into his own hands.

On the day the man was laid to rest, crowds gathered outside the gates of the cemetery in celebration of his death. These crowds were friends and supporters of the victim.

"*Justice!*" they cried.

It seemed very odd, indeed, that those who cried out for justice did not understand the difference between their goal and vengeance. Stranger still was the fact that the man's crime was the result of his own misguided attempt to find that much vaulted justice. He, too, had not understood that his own need for vengeance was not really justice at all. It was ironic that the crowds did not see that parallel as they rejoiced in the man's death.

These people; this crowd; they did not know or understand the full story having only been privy to what they heard on their televisions or read in their newspapers.

But I knew. Having heard Alejandro's confession (no, not Alejandro, but Hector, I must keep reminding myself) having heard Hector's confession, I knew the truth. Having finally met and spoken with Junior's mother and sister, I now knew the entire story.

These people, the ones who howled for their vengeance simply did not understand. When would mankind finally learn that vengeance does not belong to man?

"Vengeance is mine, so saith the Lord," and He says such for one reason: only He can know the full story.

I stood nearby the man's gravesite as they lowered his body into his final resting place and watched the very small gathering of mourners.

I looked to the man's mother and saw the stony face of anguish. Here was a woman who knew of the evils her son had perpetrated, but still mourned the loss of her child.

I looked to the man's wife and saw the silent tears that rolled down her cheek. Here was a woman who knew the man had committed a horrendous crime, but who still mourned the loss of a husband.

I looked at the face of his child; a young boy who would never understand what evil his father had wrought; a young boy who did not care. All the child knew was that his father was gone — he had a daddy no more.

And as I listened to the rejoicing outside the cemetery gates, I looked to the face of the boy. His eyes filled with tears and his face contorted in pain.

But, in those eyes, I saw something else.

I saw hatred.

I saw anger.

I saw rage.

Looking through those eyes, I did not see a boy at all. I saw wrath, and I saw fury.

And as the din of the crowd outside the gates became louder; as the voices of the angry mob grew more strident, I swear that I saw her!

I swear that I looked at that boy, I looked at the child and I saw his very essence rent into two. From the broken essence, I saw a black fury that rose into the air and hovered above the crowd. I saw that fury then disperse in hundreds of smaller pieces. I watched as those hundreds of pieces flew over and past the cemetery gates and then into the mob outside. And I watched as each tiny piece, each part of that greater fury entered into each and every single person gathered.

And as I looked into the faces of the protesters, faces contorted in anger and hatred, I was horrified to see that from each and every pair of eyes, *La Furia* stared back at me.

ABOUT THE AUTHOR

Mario Kiefer has a keen interest in people and likes to write about the things that make people tick — those hidden motivations they often do not see themselves. Although born in Austin, Texas, he has lived in many parts of the country and is fascinated by the differing cultural viewpoints he has encountered always asking himself "why"?

ALSO BY MARIO KIEFER

The Ordinary Life

The Ordinary Doll

A Collection of Monkeys

www.ingramcontent.com/pod-product-compliance
Lightning Source LLC
Chambersburg PA
CBHW020316200626
46814CB00006BA/2265